THE PONY DETECTIVES

Moonlight:
Star of the Show

First published in the UK in 2012 by Templar Publishing,

an imprint of The Templar Company Limited,

Deepdene Lodge, Deepdene Avenue, Dorking, Surrey, RH5 4AT, UK

www.templarco.co.uk

Copyright © 2012 by Belinda Rapley

Cover design by Will Steele

Illustrations by Debbie Clark

Cover photo by Samantha Lamb

4 6 8 10 9 7 5

Printed and bound by CPI Group (UK) Ltd, Croydon, CR0 4YY

THE PONY DETECTIVES

Book One

Moonlight:
Star of the Show

by Belinda Rapley

templar

For Mump and Pud

Rosie and Dancer

Mia and Wish

Alice and Scout

Charlie and Pirate

Chapter One

THE four girls rode in single file down a narrow, rocky path in the woods. Charlie and her dark bay native pony, Pirate, were in front, leading the others. Pirate, whose bushy black forelock almost covered his white star and mischievous eyes, bounced sideways excitedly as Charlie sat lightly in the saddle.

"Can you believe it? The day we've been dreaming about for ages is finally here!" She smiled, closing her eyes for a second. She kept her reins loose, knowing that if she shortened them Pirate would use that as a signal to charge off. Charlie twisted in the saddle to look back at the other three riding behind her. "We've got six whole weeks of summer holidays ahead of us.

I reckon we should make some plans – any ideas?"

"My plan is to do nothing apart from lots of hacking," Rosie piped up from the back of the ride. Suddenly she was pulled out of the saddle as her strawberry roan cob, Dancer, dived for some grass at the edge of the path. They were riding downhill and Rosie squeaked as she started to slide down her pony's neck before scrambling back into the saddle. "I thought that's what holidays were for."

"I really need to practise my showjumping," Alice said, going cold. Part of her was over the moon that it was the start of the school holidays. The other part felt like she'd swallowed a lead weight. "The Fratton Show's only one week away. I've entered Scout into the Cup but I've hardly schooled him since Easter."

The Fratton Show was the first big event of the summer holidays. It had lots of different classes all day, from gymkhana games to 'pony with the biggest ears', but the highlight was definitely the Fratton Cup. It was a huge show-jumping class which was held last on the day, and it always drew the biggest crowds. Scout, the sturdy dappled grey gelding Alice had on loan, loved jumping. So did Alice. But the crowds and the atmosphere at competitions never failed to reduce her to a bag of nerves.

"Well, I know what *I'm* doing," Mia announced as she held her palomino part-bred Arab, Wish Me Luck, with a light contact on her reins. Wish picked her way down the slope carefully. "Getting Wish prepared to win, again, in the Ridden Show Pony class next week."

Showing was Mia's speciality. Unlike the Fratton Cup, no jumps were involved in a showing class. Instead of having to clear a twisting course of brightly coloured fences, Mia had to impress the judge with her and Wish's smartness, style and correctness as they were inspected both standing still and during an individual ridden display. The pair of them ruled the local show ring, and it seemed as if Wish, with her silky palomino coat and delicately dished face, just had to place one expensive, well-oiled hoof inside it to be handed the red winner's rosette.

The four girls and their ponies reached the bottom of the rocky path and splashed across a shallow stream that gushed under the arch of a little stone bridge. Pirate charged through the water. He let out a squeal of excitement as soon as his boxy black hooves touched the soft, wooded path on the other side, and he shot off in a scurry of short legs. Alice kept her reins tight until Mia and Rosie had reached the bank too, with Scout bouncing beneath her, straining to race after Pirate. As soon as Rosie shouted that she was clear of the stream Alice softened her hold on the reins. Scout sat back on his haunches, motionless for a second, then flew forward.

Alice watched Scout's dappled neck stretch out in front of her. She listened to his fast, rhythmical hoof beats on the mossy earth as they galloped through patches of warm sunlight. His ears were pricked forward and Alice knew her pony was enjoying himself as much as she was.

Charlie, Alice then Mia breathlessly brought their ponies to a walk one after the other at the top of the hill, beaming as they trotted out of the shaded woods into the sun. Pirate backed up excitedly, hardly able to stand still for a second as Wish and Scout shook their heads, nodding them up and down and jinking their bits as they waited for Rosie. Dancer's chestnut head with its white blaze emerged slowly at the top of the sloping track. Dancer had a chestnut mane, tail and legs, but her barrel-like body was a mixture of white and chestnut hairs, making her look pink. Her saucer-like hooves thudded the ground, and she looked highly offended at being expected to canter uphill. She was determined to snatch mouthfuls of tree or shrub as she trundled her way towards them, grinding to a halt despite Rosie flapping her legs to encourage her on.

"I don't know about the rest of the holidays, but the first thing I'm going to do when I get back to the stables", Rosie said, her cheeks glowing, "is eat lunch. I'm *starving*."

Mia rolled her big, dark eyes. "Honestly, Rosie, you're as bad as Dancer. Always thinking about food."

Rosie muttered that she'd rather be eating it than thinking about it as the four girls set off to ride home at a relaxed, tail-swinging walk. They let their reins slip through their fingers so their ponies could stretch their necks, and dangled their feet out of their stirrups. By the time the ponies had wandered up the long, dusty farm track and reached the gates of Blackberry Farm, they'd cooled down.

Rosie's parents had inherited Blackberry Farm from an ancient aunt over a year ago. The farm consisted of a yellow-painted cottage, a small, rundown yard, a few big barns and acres of paddocks. As soon as they'd moved in, Rosie's parents agreed to Mia and Charlie stabling their ponies in the yard. The farm was nearer to where they both lived than their last yard, so it was perfect. They'd finally agreed to Rosie having her own pony, too, and soon afterwards Dancer had arrived, goggle-eyed and whinnying. Just a week later Alice had taken Scout on loan and she'd led him straight to the farm. Suddenly, the yard was transformed into life. Rosie's mum, an artist, had only made one condition: that the girls all took full responsibility for their ponies and the yard. The girls had agreed excitedly at once.

The yard had eight wooden stables, four of which were being used by the ponies. One of the others had been converted into a feed room, one a tack room and one had all the mucking-out tools in it. The last stable was spare. Only the four of them kept their ponies there, and they all agreed that it was pony heaven.

Charlie opened the squeaky wooden gate with its crooked hand-painted sign and clattered onto the small sunny square yard with its flowering weeds sprouting up from the cracks in the concrete. The girls were greeted by the squawking of chickens and the welcoming yaps of Beanie, Rosie's Jack Russell, who trotted importantly beside them.

They led their ponies across the yard to their stables. Scout dozed quietly outside his stable in the warm sunshine, resting one back leg as Alice undid his girth and lifted his saddle off. She put it over the stable door then reached up and slid his bridle over his ears, making sure the metal bit didn't clonk against his teeth. She slung the bridle over the saddle then slipped Scout's headcollar on and tied the lead rope to a bit of baler twine outside the stable. She dug out some mints from her pocket. Scout picked them off her hand softly, his whiskers tickling her. He shook his head up and down, crunching the mints, while Alice got a bucket and sponged his warm neck and back with some cool water.

Next she ran her hands down each of Scout's legs. Scout picked up each hoof in turn and Alice used her hoof pick to scrape them out. She turned the hoof pick over and used the brush on the other side to swish away the last of the mud.

"Come on, slow coach," Charlie called over. Alice looked up. The other three were all waiting for her, their ponies untied and ready to be turned out.

"I'm coming, hang on," Alice puffed, throwing her hoof pick into her grooming kit and hastily pulling the rope loose. She was always the last of the four to be ready although she could never work out why. She jogged over to the others waiting at the gate. Scout walked fast behind her, sticking his neck out, and they led the ponies together along the grassy path to the paddock at the back of the yard.

Pirate galloped off as soon as his headcollar was unbuckled and slipped off his nose. He bucked and wheeled, squealing and tucking his chunky neck into his chest. Wish stood looking out to the horizon, her long lashes framing her huge dark eyes as if she were posing for a photograph, ignoring Pirate's antics. Scout circled a patch of grass, his legs buckling. He chose a spot then dropped to the ground and rolled vigorously, grunting. He stood back up and shook himself before settling down to graze. Dancer twisted her head through the bottom rung of the fencing, tugging at the longer, lusher grass just outside the paddock.

As soon as the gate was clicked shut the four girls wandered over to the hay barn, where the sunlight shot through the wooden slatted walls in shafts, picking up all the dust hanging in the still air. The sweet-smelling hay made it the best place on the yard to hang out. They'd turned it into their den, with faded posters pulled from *Pony Mad*, their favourite magazine, stuck all over the walls. It was snug in the winter and cool in the summer and provided the perfect place for them to relax and keep an eye on their ponies at the same time, because the huge barn doors looked directly onto the paddock. They'd pulled bales into a circle near the barn doors among all the spilt hay and straw that made the floor spongy to walk on.

Beanie suddenly appeared in the barn, snuffling among the hay, pretending to chase rats.

"Okay, so apart from getting ready for the show next week," Charlie said, "does anyone have any other ideas for the holidays?" Neither she nor Pirate were keen on schooling. Her lightning-quick, intelligent bay pony only had two speeds, jog and flat out, and going round in circles didn't seem to improve the situation much, so the thought of schooling all week wasn't exactly filling her with joy. Charlie flopped down onto one of the straw bales, tucking her long, gangly legs up beside her. She scruffily pushed her elfin-cut dark brown hair out of her tanned face and green eyes.

Mia frowned. Any kind of untidiness in the

others bugged her. She was tall and striking, with slim legs that were always wrapped in a selection of pink or purple jodhpurs. Even after the two-hour ride that morning, Mia didn't have a single long straight black hair out of place, her olive skin was dirt free, and the tiny bit of make-up on her dark, almond-shaped eyes was still intact. Even her jodhpurs were as clean as when she'd arrived that morning. She always looked immaculate. While the others couldn't figure out her secret for staying so clean, she could never work out how they attracted so much dirt and messiness without even trying. She looked around the others as they got comfy in the barn, and sighed.

Alice was suffering from a bad case of hat hair. Her shoulder-length mousy brown hair was stuck to her head and Scout had rubbed against her pale blue T-shirt, covering it with white hair and dirty smudges. Alice was the smallest of the four girls, and her jods were always too baggy and worn because she preferred to spend any spare money she managed to save on Scout, rather than on herself. Rosie, on the other hand, was plump and somehow always managed to wear clothes that were a size too small for her. Rosie's thick, long straw-blonde hair was flyaway; she never tied it back and it floated all over the place. She was a total English rose, with pale skin, pink cheeks and blue eyes. Mia used to threaten her with a makeover, seeing how pretty she was beneath all the scatty hair and odd-shaped clothes. But Rosie was more interested in grooming Dancer than in grooming herself, and Mia had declared her a lost cause.

Looking from Charlie's spiked-up fringe, to Rosie biting her sandwich and taking a mouthful of hair with it, to Alice trying to piece together a hole in the knee of her ancient jodhpurs, Mia said that it was no wonder she was the only one of the four who went in for showing.

"None of you would ever be smart enough," she sighed.

"Or care enough about being smart," Rosie pointed out as she slumped on one of the bales. Beanie circled a couple of times before settling at her feet, rolling over to have his tummy tickled. Rosie took another big bite of her sandwich, flicking through her brand-new copy of *Pony Mad* magazine.

"Well, if anyone else fancies doing some jump schooling, we could always build a course in the paddock," Alice said half-heartedly. In the corner of the schooling paddock there was a pile of old flaking poles, some barrels and jump wings. But just the thought of putting up the jumps reminded her again of the show. Her stomach churned and she put down her apple, unable to take another bite.

"Count me out," Rosie replied, not taking her eyes off the magazine. "Sounds too much like hard work. Anyway, there's no point. I know me and Dancer will be totally useless in the Cup, however much jumping practice we have.

Last year we had two refusals and got eliminated at the first fence."

She looked up for a second, starting to giggle with Alice and Charlie as they remembered Dancer deciding to stop and eat the decorative shrubs beside the first fence, rather than jump it. After Rosie's third failed attempt to get her over, Dancer had left the ring with one of the shrubs hanging from her clenched teeth.

"There's really no need to remind us of that painful experience," Mia sighed. "Don't you even want to try to get a rosette this year?"

"Er, no. I'm not ultra competitive like you, Mia," Rosie replied, opening a packet of crisps with a pop. "I'll go in for the class again because Dancer enjoys a day out, but I'm not bothered about winning anything. I'm just as happy hacking about. Anyway, I'd rather be realistic about my riding than be like Alice."

"What's that supposed to mean?" Alice asked indignantly as she stopped reading over Rosie's shoulder the *Pony Mad* article about how to ride the perfect circle.

"She means that at least she doesn't almost die of nerves before each show," Charlie explained. "Face it, Alice, you're already as jumpy as a flea and there's still a week to go before the Fratton Cup."

Charlie was right. Even hearing the words 'Fratton Cup' said out loud made Alice's knees turn to jelly.

"I don't get it," Alice replied. "How come you never worry about competing?"

"Because there's no need to, that's why," Charlie said, as if it were the most obvious thing in the world. "We go to the show, Pirate either clears every fence or knocks them all down depending on what mood he's in, then we go home. Simple."

Alice sighed, wondering if she'd ever be as brave as Charlie. Charlie had been riding for ever, and she'd owned Pirate for years. They knew each other inside out, and although none of the other three dared sit on him, Alice knew that, for Charlie, Pirate was the best pony ever. He was a daredevil who'd tackle anything, just like her. The only worry Charlie ever talked about was outgrowing Pirate. He was 13.2 hands high, and she had suddenly started to shoot up.

Alice, on the other hand, worried about everything. Because Pirate was shorter than Scout and Dancer, he'd be competing in a different class, with smaller fences. Alice wished for a second that she could shrink Scout, just for the day. She knew the fences for the Cup would be huge, with tall uprights and vast spreads. Last year she'd been eliminated when her mind went blank halfway round and she'd taken the wrong course. Despite this, Alice still couldn't stop herself dreaming of winning the Cup one day.

"Well, I think it's pretty clear who'll take first place," Mia remarked matter-of-factly, crunching on a carrot stick. "Poppy Brookes. She's bound to win again. Moonlight's totally amazing. They've won for the last two years in a row and I can't see anyone beating them."

"Not even Tallulah Starr?" Rosie asked. "She's got a whole string of good jumping ponies. She *must* be one of Poppy's biggest rivals."

"The Starr ponies are good," Mia said, thinking about Tallulah's team of grey ponies and the entourage of grooms she had to help keep them sparkling. "But they can't quite match Moonlight over a fence. And Tallulah isn't anywhere near as skilful as Poppy in the saddle."

"What about Mark Tickle, then?" Charlie suggested. "He was runner-up to Poppy both times so he'll be desperate to win this year. You know what he's like – he's so competitive, it's almost unsportsmanlike. I bet he's sitting in his yard right now trying to come up with a plan to topple her."

"No," Mia replied sitting up. "Poppy and Moonlight are in a league of their own. I bet you my favourite pink jodhpurs that Poppy wins again this year, no matter what Mark or Tallulah do."

"Oh no, she won't!" Rosie gasped, inhaling a crisp the wrong way by mistake. She started to choke, and in between big gulps of air spluttered, "She can't!"

"What are you on about?" Charlie asked as she thumped her on the back.

"Look!" she whispered hoarsely, jabbing a greasy finger at a photo in the classifieds at the back of her magazine. "It's Moonlight! There, in the 'Missing' section!"

They all stared in silence, unable to take it in. Up until now it had been as if the ponies in the 'Missing' photos were somehow not real. But they knew Moonlight. He was stabled not that far from Blackberry Farm and was a celebrity on the local showjumping circuit.

"Read out the ad," Mia said as they all leaned in.

Rosie cleared her throat and put on her serious voice: "Piebald showjumping pony stolen from paddock. 14.2 hands high, twelve years, answers to name of Moonlight. Please call Poppy if you have any information."

They tried to imagine coming into the yard one day and finding that overnight their ponies had mysteriously disappeared, the awfulness of seeing a stable door open and no pony inside. The worst would be not knowing what had happened, or how their ponies were being treated and wondering if they'd ever get to see them again. It was terrifying and impossible. And with the Fratton Show coming up, the timing couldn't have been worse – Poppy must be shattered.

Rosie suddenly perked up.

"Ooh, I wonder if they're offering a reward?"

The others all glared at her.

"I was just saying!" she added huffily, turning back to her magazine and flicking the page.

"Well, that's it then," Charlie sighed. "Mark will

finally get the first place he's so desperate for in the Cup."

"Ooh, ooh, ooh!" Rosie said, her blue eyes wide. "Maybe *he* stole Moonlight so that he could win. I wonder if I should call Poppy and suggest that. Then I could ask her if there's a reward going at the same time."

"Maybe Rosie's got a point," Alice said suddenly.

Mia and Charlie looked at her as if she were mad.

"I don't mean about the reward, or calling Poppy – but her yard isn't far away," she explained. "Moonlight might've been stolen by someone near here. I know! Why don't we try to find him? I mean, imagine if it was one of our ponies – I know I'd feel terrible, and I'd want everyone around to be searching for Scout if he went missing."

Charlie frowned for a second; it sounded like a crazy idea. Then suddenly her eyes lit up as she realised what looking for Moonlight might involve. "Yes! We'll get to gallop all over the place, checking every paddock and every stable for possible clues!"

"Think how much chocolate we could buy if there is a reward!" Rosie said, getting excited too. The pair of them started to jump up and down around the barn, holding onto each other's arms. Beanie joined in too, leaping up and bouncing between them as if he were on springs, yapping and adding to the general noise.

"I might get my picture in this magazine! They might do a whole feature on me... I mean us!" Mia gasped, looking at the pages of *Pony Mad* reverently.

"We'll be famous super sleuths!" Rosie shouted.

"Right, come on then, we need a plan," Mia said, clapping her hands and bringing the others to order as her mind raced with the possibilities of photos and fame.

"First we'll have to visit Poppy's yard, Hawthorn Farm. It's about four miles away, I think," Alice said loudly, hardly able to control her voice she was so delighted with her idea. "The ponies can't go out again today, so we'll have to wait till tomorrow to start the investigation. That'll give me time to find a map."

The others nodded in agreement.

"I'll get a notebook and pen," Mia said seriously, "to write down all the clues in."

"I'll organise snacks – if the yard's that far away we'll need them," Rosie added even more seriously. "And we'd better take sandwiches, too."

"OK, so tomorrow we ride out to Hawthorn Farm and search for clues," Mia said, before starting to smile. "Imagine how happy Poppy will be if we manage to find Moonlight before the Fratton Show!"

"That doesn't give us long, though." Charlie frowned.

"Exactly. The next week will have to be

crammed with frantic evidence-gathering," Alice said enthusiastically.

"And lots of galloping between one bit of evidence-gathering and the next," Charlie reminded her, thinking how much Pirate would absolutely love that. Not a schooling circle in sight!

"I say we get going at ten o'clock tomorrow morning," Mia said.

"Right, that's sorted, then," Rosie nodded.

"Settled," Charlie agreed, and they all stood up, gathered the rubbish from their packed lunches and marched out of the den, fired with a new purpose.

Alice hastily picked up the apple she was saving for Scout and rushed after them. A thought suddenly struck her. In all the excitement she'd completely forgotten about her own plans for the next week. Her stomach lurched again as she thought about how little time there was both to school Scout and to find Moonlight. The show was looming closer by the hour. Alice called Scout and he came trotting over, his ears pricked as he scuffed to a messy halt by the paddock fence, snorting. As she held the apple out on her hand Alice noticed that it was already starting to shake.

THE next day Rosie stepped out of Blackberry Farm cottage just as Alice and Charlie pedalled up. The two lived in the same street, in the same village not far from the farm, and during the light summer mornings they called for each other at 7.30 a.m. then cycled to the yard together. As they dumped their bikes just outside the gate, Mia's dad rolled up in his car and Mia jumped out looking a totally fresh vision in pink as the others yawned and tried to wake up. They crossed the yard and picked the headcollars from the hooks outside each of their stables, then walked towards the turnout paddock.

The four ponies were waiting at the gate. As soon as they saw the girls they set up a chorus of whinnies in greeting. Dancer jostled the other ponies as Rosie slipped on her headcollar, keen to get back to the yard – and her breakfast – before the others. Alice climbed the gate and slid onto Scout's warm, silky back and Charlie vaulted onto Pirate from the ground. They rode their ponies up to the yard bareback, while Mia and Rosie led Wish and Dancer.

They tied up their ponies outside the stables in the cool early sunshine and quickly mixed their feeds. Dancer scraped the concrete with a front hoof, demanding her breakfast, until Rosie rushed over with her bucket.

"Honestly, Dancer, all that fuss over a handful of pony nuts," Rosie yawned.

As the ponies slurped and sloshed their feeds the girls fetched their grooming kits from the tack room and started to brush their ponies.

"I'm convinced that all grooming ever does is shift grime from Pirate onto me," Charlie commented with a frown, looking from her bay pony's summer coat, which shone like a polished conker, with his black points over his knees and hocks gleaming, to her own pale green T-shirt and slightly too-short purple jodhpurs. They were already streaked with dirt.

Once the ponies were sparkling and enough time had passed after they'd been fed, the girls tacked up. They set off filled with excitement and armed with a map and Mia's notebook. Their pockets were stuffed with cereal bars and already squashed sandwiches for them and apples, carrots and mints for the ponies. As they left the back of the yard, the ponies started out down the usual well-worn route – past the turnout paddock and onto the bridleway that led through the woods beyond. They took the path to the left, with Pirate pulling at his reins, a bundle of endless energy jig-jogging all the way.

The bridleway took them to the end of the woods and they cantered along the grassy edge of a field filled with shimmering golden wheat.

At the end of the field they rode onto a dirt track and Charlie unfolded the map to check where to go next.

"Down this way," she announced, turning Pirate right along the track, which led onto a small, winding lane covered by the shade of overhanging branches. Once they'd left their familiar path, Pirate stopped playing up and his small, hard ears pricked alertly as he bobbed along at the head of the group. Charlie's legs dangled below Pirate's elbows, her feet out of the stirrups.

They kept a lookout for a bridleway marked on the map that crossed a big field. They soon found the field but the map hadn't warned them that it would be filled with cows. The cows crowded round in spite of the girls shooing them, clinging to the ponies and jostling them while Rosie dragged the gate shut across the thick grass. Scout shied nervously, then suddenly bolted. From the squeals and thudding hooves that Alice heard behind her, she guessed her pony wasn't the only one.

For a second Alice felt out of control as Scout thundered along. She grabbed a handful of mane, then she relaxed and leaned forward, lifting her weight out of the saddle and enjoying the exhilaration of speed. Suddenly Pirate was at her shoulder, racing Scout. Charlie grinned at Alice before Scout's stride started to shorten and Alice began to pull him up as they reached the gate at the far end of the field.

"Where's Rosie?" Alice shouted, looking round and seeing Charlie cantering Pirate in a large circle to slow him down. Wish wasn't far behind, looking gee'ed up by the gallop, unlike Mia, who was as cool as ever on top. Mia looked round too. That's when they realised – only three of them had made it.

Suddenly they heard a high-pitched squeal.

"Can't one of you *please* help me?"

At first it was as if Rosie's voice were coming from inside one of the cows, and Charlie wondered out loud whether she and Dancer had been swallowed by one. But when they looked closer they saw that there, stuck in the middle of the herd of bustling cream Jerseys, was Rosie. Dancer was progressing slowly, her neck stretched upwards and her goggly eyes out on stalks, snorting wildly with every stride.

By the time the girls had stopped laughing and were thinking about going to help, the cows had lost interest and wandered away.

"Thanks a bunch!" Rosie said indignantly as she finally reached them. "Some friends *you* are!"

"Er, Rosie," Charlie said between big gulps of air, wiping the tears of laughter from her eyes, "what's all that... that browny green stuff splattered all over you?"

Mia leaned closer. She sniffed.

"Ugh!" she cried, pinching her nose dramatically. "It's cowpat!"

Charlie and Alice collapsed into fresh fits of laughter.

"Well, it was your fault! It was your ponies

that kicked it up as you all galloped off and *left me*!" Rosie protested, trying hard not to laugh now herself.

She started to scrape the offending splats off with her whip but that just smeared them. There were even some long, straggly lumps in her hair.

After that Mia refused point blank to ride near Rosie, insisting she take the lead with Dancer relegated to last. The ponies trotted along another couple of quiet lanes, their metallic clip-clopping the only noise apart from the constant birdsong until they turned off and headed onto a huge, gently sloping grassy hill. The ponies stretched out their necks and flew to the top. From there they rode into some woods where the ground was soft and springy under the ponies' hooves.

"Look! Jumps!" Charlie cried.

She pulled up Pirate, who backed into a bush and half reared in excitement, his chunky neck all bunched up. There, along the path in front of them, were a series of natural-looking jumps that had been set up: fallen logs, old stone walls and tyre fences. Charlie trotted to each fence quickly first to check that there weren't any bad landings, then rode back, calling out that they were safe to jump.

"See – you can school while we hack, Alice!" she cried as she turned Pirate once more. He bunny-hopped sideways for a couple of strides before taking off and disappearing into the bright, sunny woods.

Alice didn't quite see how solid fences taken at speed could be good schooling for the show-jumping ring, where control and collection were the order of the day. But she knew they'd be fun so she pressed her lower legs to Scout's warm sides and he took off towards the small fences. Alice hardly felt his stride break as he flew over the first log, then curved round the slight bend to the tyre fence, which he popped over easily. Alice patted his neck as they cantered on to the white stone wall ahead, sitting into the saddle until they reached it and then folding forward over Scout's neck. Scout stretched out over the next tyre fence and the wood pile, tucking up his hooves neatly and clearing them fluently.

As Alice pulled up, patting Scout and beaming, she rode over to the clearing where Charlie was standing. Pirate pawed the ground with his small black hoof, all fired up. Alice leaned over and held Pirate's reins near the bit, patting his damp neck, while Charlie pulled out the map and checked it. Mia had thought about not jumping Wish – she was always aware that if Wish ever cut herself over fences and got a scar it would count against her in the show ring. But she knew her mare enjoyed it, so she let her take the fences slowly. Wish elegantly cleared them and joined the others, followed by Dancer, who veered to the left at the last fence, jumping the edge of it. Rosie managed to cling on somehow, ducking to avoid being clonked by a thick, overhanging branch, and trotted over to them.

They rested the ponies in the shade and ate their

sandwiches hungrily as Charlie checked the map once more. Just as they were about to set off again along the path that led from the woods, they heard a loud voice barking instructions. The girls looked at one another and groaned – Major Thurlow.

The next second a man wearing a tweed shooting jacket, a flat cap and beige trousers marched into sight along the path. He was thwacking the bushes either side of him with a walking stick and looked menacingly determined.

"Does he think this is a jungle?" Rosie whispered as Pirate shied away and backed into Dancer, squashing Rosie's leg with a metallic clash of stirrup irons.

The Major looked up, nodded a clipped greeting to the girls, then continued with his instructions.

"Get that pony going, Daisy!" Major Thurlow roared, glancing over his shoulder. "Ride 'im like you're in charge, c'mon, sharpen up!"

A black pony emerged along the path behind

the Major. In the saddle sat a girl the same age as them. She had long brown hair and her riding hat framed a delicate, pale face. She looked utterly miserable.

"Hi, Daisy," Alice said, smiling.

"Hi," Daisy replied wanly, not meeting her gaze.

"What are you doing over here?" Rosie asked, thinking that the woods were a bit out of the way from where Daisy lived.

"Don't ask," Daisy said disconsolately, looking down at the ground.

"Now, Daisy, no time for pleasantries!" Major Thurlow, Daisy's dad, commanded. "We haven't ridden two miles from home to train out in the wilds just for you to stop and be sociable. Now, I want you to take Shadow over the fences through these woods. Ride 'im at speed! It'll do your confidence no end of good. Now, give the pony a kick and ride like you mean it!"

Daisy took a deep breath and squeezed

Shadow on. The black pony flattened his ears and swished his tail irritably.

"Don't tickle the poor beast!" the Major shouted, his jaw twitching. "You're not going to win the Fratton Cup riding like that, are you?"

"I don't even want to *ride* in the Cup, Dad, let alone win it," Daisy hissed quietly, struggling as Shadow weasled about on the path. "Just because you used to win every competition when you rode in the army, it doesn't mean that I should do the same, does it?"

"Nonsense! You've got a family reputation to keep up! You're going to win that Cup this year and show everyone what a fine rider you are!" Major Thurlow yelled. "Like father, like daughter, eh?"

With that Daisy rolled her eyes, looking thoroughly fed up, and clumped her heels to Shadow's side. The black pony jumped forward with a squeal and shot off along the path. They all watched as Shadow reached the first fence.

The sly pony ducked around it, almost unseating Daisy, then bucked and dropped his shoulder at the same time.

Mia groaned as she watched Daisy's saddle start to slip. They'd met Daisy and Shadow out on rides lots of times and on most of them Daisy had ended up on the ground after forgetting to tighten her girth. Shadow seemed to know this and would do his worst to get rid of her at every opportunity. Consequently Daisy spent more time lying down on the grass than sitting in the saddle. Once again Daisy slid to the ground and lay there with a sigh as Shadow charged back to the other ponies. He put the brakes on at the last second, skidding towards them. As Alice went to grab his reins the black pony flattened his ears, opened his mouth and clamped his teeth around her finger.

"Ow!" she yelped as the Major marched up and took charge of Shadow, shaking the pony's bridle. He scowled at the girls from under his cap.

"Your ponies put poor Daisy off, unsettling Shadow like that," he growled. "Tell me, any of you entering the Fratton Cup?"

Alice and Rosie exchanged glances and nodded slightly.

"Ha!" he exclaimed, thwacking his stick into a nearby bush and making Scout jump. "You're putting Daisy off on purpose, then! Can't stand the competition! Well, just you wait. Your tactics won't work – trust me. We've got this one in the bag! Come on, Daisy, back in the saddle. Let's try again!"

The girls watched as the Major marched Shadow towards Daisy, who was getting to her feet, her head down.

"Dad, I really don't think this is going to make much difference to my performance at the show," she muttered, trying to rearrange the saddle before her dad legged her back up.

"We'll start from the other end this time," the Major said, ignoring her and thwacking his way deeper into the woods, out of sight. The girls watched as Daisy wobbled precariously in the saddle. She half glanced behind her, then turned away and disappeared too.

"Poor Daisy," Charlie sighed. "I wouldn't want to ride Shadow – he's a total menace."

"So's her dad," Rosie added. "He should realise that teaching Daisy to jump is a bit like me trying to get Dancer airborne. It's just physically impossible and shouldn't be attempted."

"Does he *really* think she can win the Fratton Cup?" Alice asked, shaking her head.

"Talking of the Cup, we'd better get going," Mia said, remembering suddenly why they'd come out in the first place.

"Moonlight's yard, Hawthorn Farm, isn't far according to the map," Charlie said, checking it quickly. "It's just a few fields away now."

"Come on then," Rosie said, surprising Dancer into a brisk walk. "The sooner we get there, the sooner we can have a snack."

U U U U

"Look, there it is!" Charlie said as they rode across a stubble field. Ahead they saw a narrow dusty drive separating the field from a pink cottage trailed with ivy. Next to it were some paddocks mainly filled with sheep, but the one nearest the drive had a few horses in it too. Next to that paddock were about six brick stables set back beyond a gate in a small concrete yard. To the side of the yard was a concreted car park, with an old Land Rover and horse trailer standing in it.

Alice felt a tingle of excitement as they rode off the stubble field straight onto the drive. Poppy was a huge hero of hers, and here they were, at her yard, hoping to solve the mystery of her stolen pony! Suddenly a car roared past the end of the drive, followed by two more. Scout shied, and Alice noticed that the road at the end of the drive was busy, with cars passing pretty frequently just while they stood there. She glanced up in the other direction. The drive ended just past the cottage. There was a wooden signpost pointing to a bridleway that led up the drive and into a narrow path that disappeared into the woods that began where the drive finished.

As Rosie reached in her pocket and handed round cereal bars, she began to wish she'd thought to bring a magnifying glass too, so she could feel like a proper detective. A couple of the ponies in the field lifted their heads and neighed loudly. They trotted over to the fence, propping and sliding to a halt and blowing heavily through their noses in greeting. Rosie felt Dancer's sides heave as she stretched out her nose towards theirs, breathing hard. Dancer squealed, at which point Charlie suggested to Rosie that it might be wise to move her pony away before she kicked out.

After Rosie had moved a reluctant Dancer the ponies in the field lost interest, and they wandered off and carried on grazing. The girls turned their attention to their surroundings.

"The ad in *Pony Mad* said Moonlight had been stolen from his field, didn't it? I wonder if it was *this* one?" Alice whispered in awe.

"It's the only field with ponies in," Mia said, looking round at the other fields of sheep beyond. "It *has* to be the crime scene!"

"Let's look here first, then," Charlie suggested in a hushed voice. "It may hold some clues."

"Solid metal gate," Rosie said, staring at the entrance to the field.

Mia pulled out her notebook and started writing.

"Standard type," she said, chewing her lip as she concentrated.

"Padlocks and thick metal chains securing it to heavy posts either side." Charlie leaned forward in the saddle and picked up one of the shiny, new-looking heavy chains then clanked it back down again.

"Recent addition," Alice added, suddenly feeling the urge to giggle in all the serious quietness.

They squeezed their ponies towards the paddock gate and squished as close as they could to it, standing up in their stirrups and leaning forward to scour the field from the saddle. They silently raced each other to find the first proper piece of evidence, but everything looked disappointingly ordinary. There was post-and-rail fencing, but beyond that a thick hedge surrounded the field on all sides except the one they were standing by, with the gate. It was a well-hidden field, invisible from the busy road next to it.

"Look!" Rosie suddenly exclaimed loudly, shooting out of her saddle as Dancer yanked the reins through her fingers. The mare ripped out a huge clump of grass from the verge and began to shake her head, scattering mud from the roots everywhere.

The others all stared, following Rosie's finger as it waved wildly at the ground.

"What exactly are we meant to be looking at?"

Charlie asked, squinting as Mia stood with her pencil poised.

"Tracks!" Rosie said theatrically. "Lots of them!"

They all looked again. Rosie was right – there were hoof prints all over the dusty drive. And they were recent. So recent, they could have been…

"Ours," Mia said witheringly, putting her pencil down again. "Honestly, Rosie, you're hopeless."

Charlie and Alice shoved their gloved fingers in their mouths to stop themselves collapsing into fits of giggles. Pirate, taking advantage of Charlie's moment of weakness, darted forward, bored with standing around. Charlie almost did a backwards roll, arms and legs flying in every direction, before falling to the ground in a dust-covered heap. Alice fell back onto Scout's rump and laughed out loud.

"Can I help you?"

Alice stopped laughing in an instant, sat bolt upright and turned to see a grey-haired woman with a severe face standing by the yard gate, staring at the four girls suspiciously. They knew from seeing the woman at shows that she was Poppy's mum. Alice wished instantly that she'd taken the trouble to pick out all the bits of mud from Scout's flowing tail. Rosie, covered with cowpat smears, turned bright pink as Dancer raised her head, a grass ball with a clod of mud attached to it hanging from her mouth. Charlie picked herself up from the ground, coated with dust. Only Mia, in her electric pink T-shirt, lilac gilet and bright purple checked jodhpurs, looked respectable. She glanced over at the others critically before taking it upon herself to be the spokesperson for the untidy gang.

"I'm sorry to disturb you, it's just that we keep our ponies nearby – at Blackberry Farm – and we know Moonlight from seeing him at shows. We read about him being stolen and thought we might be able to help, if we knew a bit more about what happened," she said, trying to sound professional. "We were wondering if any tack was stolen with him?"

Mia kept very calm even though the other three were starting to crack under the icy looks they were getting.

"No, it wasn't," Poppy's mum replied. She peered a bit closer, then marched up to Wish and Mia. Suddenly her face softened and she smiled slightly. "Hang on, it's Mia, isn't it? I recognise your pony. Wins a lot in the showing ring, doesn't she?"

Mia couldn't help but smile smugly and nod.

"Wait there a moment," Poppy's mum said.

She disappeared into the yard and spoke to someone in the tack room. A girl came to the door a second later with drooping shoulders, her face pale. The four of them recognised her at once – it was Poppy Brookes, Moonlight's owner.

Mia raised her hand and forced a cheerful smile. Poppy knew Mia to say hello to – she was as much of a celebrity locally in the show ring as Poppy was in the showjumping world – but as Poppy tried to smile back, seeing the four of them standing there with their ponies, her face crumpled and she ran back into the tack room. As her mum stalked back out, Alice thought she saw a bit of dirt on Scout's reins and tried to clean it off with her nail.

"Listen, it's very kind of you to try to help, and if you do see anything please let me know," she said, "but I hope you realise how serious this is for Poppy."

With that she went into the cottage next to the yard, calling Poppy to have a lemonade. As she left the tack room, Poppy wiped her nose and looked over at the girls, half waving a goodbye as if she was trying to say thank you without having to speak in case she got choked up again.

Alice felt herself go red and patted Scout as she turned him round. It struck her as she felt his warm, sturdy neck beneath her fingers that Moonlight was as real a pony as Scout, and with a rush she suddenly knew what it would be like if that feeling was taken away for ever. She'd had Scout on loan for just over a year after falling in love with him when she caught sight of him wandering on the marshes, thin and neglected. His owner had agreed to loan him and Alice knew already that her life would never be the same if he wasn't around. He was everything to her, her best friend in the whole world.

She guessed everyone else was feeling the same because after Charlie swung into the saddle they headed back to Blackberry Farm in silence.

Chapter Three

"Maybe we should just give up," Rosie sighed as she collapsed onto a hay bale in the den, rubbing Beanie behind his ears.

"No way," Charlie replied, quick as a flash.

Although no one had said anything, it was pretty clear as they looked round at one another that they were all thinking the same thing: that the case was hopeless and Moonlight would most probably be miles away by now. But that didn't mean they could just give up, whatever the odds were of actually finding Moonlight.

After the visit to Hawthorn Farm, somehow they all seemed to understand that looking for Poppy's pony was no longer a game, or a way to get a reward or to appear in a magazine. It was something they had to do. It felt as desperate as if it was one of their own ponies that had been stolen.

"I agree," Mia sniffed, pulling out her notebook. Her eyes looked slightly red from where she'd been wiping them as they'd ridden back. "Let's look at what we've got so far."

They all gathered round. Mia had stuck in the 'missing' advert from *Pony Mad* at the top of the page. Underneath she had written, in her neat handwriting:

Clue 1
Solid metal gate, standard. New padlocks on there - maybe put on since the theft of Moonlight?

Clue 2
No tack was stolen with Moonlight.

Clue 3
Tracks on the pa...

"It's not much to go on," Charlie said, trying hard not to sound disappointed. Alice kept staring at the page. She couldn't help thinking that they were missing something but couldn't work out what. Then she jumped up.

"I've got it!" she cried, so loudly that even Scout started out in the field. "Rosie was right!"

Everyone looked up at Alice expectantly.

"I knew it!" Rosie said proudly, a grin spreading all over her round, pink-cheeked face. Then she frowned. "Er, how am I right, exactly? I mean, I know I am, that much is obvious, it's just that I can't quite see…" She bent over the notebook again, scanning the few lines of handwriting. Her hair, still smelling of cowpat, fell forward and marked the page with a green streak, much to Mia's disgust.

"I mean that your observation about the tracks might not be so useless after all. In fact, it might prove crucial to our investigation." Alice paced up and down as she thought. "Because when we looked at the lane, there *were* hoof prints everywhere in the dusty pathway."

"Lots of hoof prints," Rosie nodded enthusiastically, "but I still don't get how that's a clue…"

"Well, it's not so much the hoof prints themselves," Alice explained. "It's just that we were so busy looking at them that we didn't think about tyre tracks, did we?"

Alice absently picked up the ginger yard cat, Pumpkin, as he rubbed purring around her legs.

"So?" Charlie asked, confused. "What about them?"

"Well, that drive was only short, wasn't it?" Alice said, frowning as she thought hard but starting to feel a buzz of excitement at the same time. "At one end was a seriously busy road, at the other a narrow bridleway into the woods. The only place to have loaded Moonlight into a trailer or a horsebox would have been right outside the yard."

"And there's no way that could have been done without making loads of noise!" Mia said, catching on and nodding. "Either from the engine or from Moonlight's hooves clattering up the ramp!"

"So he must have been *led* away," Alice said, getting wildly enthusiastic, "either up the little bridleway into the woods or the way we came – across the stubble field."

"And it must have been at night, when no one was around to see," added Charlie.

They grabbed the map, laid it out flat on the floor of the barn and studied it. The busy road went on for ages, with lots of twists and bends and no turn-offs.

"And *that* must mean that whoever took him was local," Mia said, her pen scratching fast to keep up with all the ideas flying round, "because they must have known they'd have to lead him away on foot."

Alice nodded. "Which must mean they couldn't have taken him *that* far."

"And remember," Charlie added, getting excited, "that field was completely cut off from sight nearly all around. I mean, you wouldn't just stumble across it, or be able to pick out a good pony as you drove past. This wasn't a random theft, it *can't* have been!"

"Exactly – Moonlight *must* have been taken by someone local," Alice said. "Someone who knew how talented he was..."

Mia looked up, her eyes wide. "So Moonlight was targeted!"

"It's starting to look that way," Charlie said. "But why?"

"And who by?" Alice added.

They were silent for a second.

"Oh, I know! I've got it!" Rosie started to giggle. "I've *got* it!"

"Who?" Charlie asked, hardly daring to, knowing from the look on Rosie's pink face as she giggled that it had to be someone ridiculous.

"It must have been Daisy!" Rosie squeaked.

Charlie laughed behind her hand. "Of course! The barmy Major's determined she'll win the Cup. Maybe he just needed to get his hands on the best pony in the area to prove he's right, even though poor Daisy keeps telling him that she doesn't even *like* jumping!"

Alice was about to giggle but the look on Mia's face silenced her at once.

"Listen, you lot, we really don't have time to mess about, so can we please take this seriously and concentrate on proper suggestions? Even though Moonlight must have been taken by someone local that doesn't mean he's still in the area. But, on the slim chance that he is, we need to think about who has fields and yards nearby."

Charlie wiped her eyes and looked away from Rosie, who was still desperately trying to control her giggling fit behind Mia.

"I know – what about a local horse dealer?" Charlie said in a high voice before clearing her throat. "They'd have ponies going in and out all the time so a new one arriving out of nowhere wouldn't cause a stir."

"Ooh – what about Harry Franklin? He's got a yard close to Hawthorn Farm," Rosie suggested. "Mum and Dad went there to look for a pony before we found Dancer. They didn't hang around long, though – said he seemed a bit rough and scary."

"I wonder if he gets asked by people to find specific ponies," Mia mused.

"Maybe he's stealing to order!" Alice gasped as she looked round wildly at everyone's excited faces. "Someone asks him for an awesome show jumper and he knows exactly where to find one!"

Suddenly it felt as if they were really starting to get somewhere.

"We need to pay this Harry Franklin a visit," Mia said darkly.

"Agreed, only not today," Rosie replied, standing up and stretching. "Mum's cooking my favourite tonight – shepherd's pie – I can almost smell it, so I can't be late getting back to the cottage..."

Mia rolled her eyes, but when she checked her watch they realised that it was nearly five o'clock.

As they caught the ponies and led them back round to the yard in the hazy late afternoon sun, everyone agreed they would set off to Harry Franklin's yard the next day. Before she left, Alice gave Scout a special evening feed with heaps of extra carrots and apples mixed in with the chaff, molasses and pony nuts. Looking sideways, she noticed the others quietly doing the same too.

Scout dived in greedily, waving his front hoof as he slurped and munched. He didn't know why he'd deserved the bumper feed, but he was delighted with it. After he'd finished Alice hugged him goodnight, smelling his sweet breath over her face. As she turned him back out into the field for the night, she wished for the first time ever that she could keep him padlocked in a stable, safe from any silent thieves who might visit.

As Mia's dad arrived in his huge sleek car to

collect her, she waved goodbye to the others and Rosie disappeared inside the sunny yellow cottage, closely followed by Beanie and Pumpkin. Charlie and Alice picked up their battered bikes and left the yard reluctantly. Even Rosie promising to sleep with her curtains open hadn't made them feel any easier.

"Probably because she's the heaviest sleeper…" Charlie began, starting to smile.

"… *and* the loudest snorer out of all of us!" Alice cut in.

Alice and Charlie started to laugh as they pedalled home in the early evening, looking forward to the next day.

Chapter Four

"So, what do we do now?" Rosie asked, pink-faced and harassed as Dancer pulled hard on her reins, diving for a particularly tasty-looking bit of hedge. They'd managed to fit in two long gallops and the jumps through the wood that they'd found the day before on the way over to Harry Franklin's. Now they'd dismounted and were loitering in a field that overlooked the dealer's sprawling yard and paddocks, positioned behind a not particularly tall hedge.

"Obvious – let's just go down there and confront him," Charlie suggested, as Pirate pawed the ground, impatient with all the hanging about.

"We can't just tell him we're looking for a stolen pony and he's our number-one suspect,"

Mia scoffed. "He'd throw us out in no time. No, we need to look round his yard without arousing suspicion."

"I don't get why we can't just stay here and keep an eye on the place," Rosie muttered, leaning against Dancer's roan neck and giving her a hug as the pony happily munched the mouthful of hedge she'd snaffled.

As they got into an argument about what to do next, Alice looked down at the yard and saw a big white horse being ridden along the lane by a huge, burly looking man not wearing a hard hat. As he turned into the drive that led to the yard, she saw him look up and figured that it must be Harry.

"Duck!" she shouted. She wasn't quite sure why, even as she obeyed her own panicky order.

The other three quickly followed, but the hedge was small and, even though they managed to hide, their four restless ponies were still highly visible from every direction, including the one from which Harry Franklin was now rapidly approaching.

Despite realising how ridiculous it was, Alice stayed down because she wasn't sure what to do next. She could feel Scout's warm, inquisitive breath on her neck and hear Charlie's muffled squeals as she gripped onto Pirate's reins and was dragged across the grass by the restless pony. Alice got as small as she could, not daring to look up. Over the sound of Dancer noisily cropping grass and munching, Alice heard hoof beats getting louder and louder until they stopped right in front of her.

"What the heck are you lot up to?" a deep, mountainous voice rumbled from high above them.

A man with a harshly bristled chin and cold, black eyes stared down at them from a massive white horse. A dog growled menacingly from the other side of the hedge. Rosie whimpered.

"Well, what do you think we're up to?" Mia suddenly took her hands from over her head, stood up and brushed the grass from her bright pink jodhpurs. Her large dark eyes looked directly back at Harry, as if it were perfectly normal to hide behind hedges. "I've come to look for a pony. Why do most people visit a dealer?"

You had to hand it to her, Mia could think on her feet. Well, her knees, actually.

"Most people who visit a dealer," Harry grumbled, looking critically at Wish, "use the front gate."

He turned the big white horse and whistled to the dog.

"Come on, Growler."

The lurcher came into view: a huge, tall dog with rough brindle fur and big, slavering jaws.

"If it's a pony you're after, you better follow me. You can jump the hedge, I take it?"

"Of course," Rosie simpered and immediately wished she hadn't said it. Dancer could probably eat her way through, but jump it?

They mounted, and with the shortest of approaches Charlie faced Pirate at the jump, flew over and galloped off down the field. Alice followed and Scout leaped it without hesitation, with an anxious Mia jumping Wish, who looked as if she was having a whale of a time, hot on Scout's heels. Behind them all Rosie flapped but Dancer slid to a goggled-eyed halt once, then twice.

"Don't just leave me!" Rosie cried, getting desperate.

Alice slowed Scout and arced him back up the hill to give Rosie a lead, but suddenly Dancer must have had the same thought as Rosie because the next second the strawberry pony took off from standstill, stag-leaping the low hedge. Rosie parted company with Dancer in mid air and landed on the other side of the hedge on her feet, much to her surprise, still hanging onto the reins. Rosie wasted no time in flinging herself back into the saddle and hung on stirrupless as Dancer whinnied loudly and raced down the hill to catch up with the others.

Once they reached the rambling, untidy yard, Harry dismounted and handed his big white horse to a tall skinny stable lad who led it to a corner stable. Harry gruffly told the girls they could tie up their ponies. Luckily Mia, ever organised, had made everyone bring their own headcollars on this ride, so they didn't have to use Harry's and risk the ponies picking up any infections.

"So, what sort of pony is it you're after?" Harry asked, staring at Wish again.

"What sort have you got?" Mia replied, casually.

"Depends what sort you're looking for."

Mia forced a smile, thinking that he was clearly going to be slippery. All they had to do now was work out whether that slipperiness was normal or if it was to do with Harry harbouring stolen ponies. Mia took a deep breath, holding her nerve.

"I'm looking for a jumping pony. I want to enter the Fratton Cup next week and show-jumping isn't Wish's strength. Better in the show ring," Mia explained, proudly pointing out her palomino. Wish raised her exquisite head on cue and looked into the distance at something no one else could see, posing beautifully.

Harry rubbed his chin with a huge, slablike hand, making a sound like sandpaper against rough wood. "You're sure it's a jumping pony you're after? Not a better show pony?"

"I don't happen to think there is a better one than Wish, actually," Mia replied, her almond eyes widening as she failed for a second to hide the irritation in her voice. "There aren't many that can match her in the show ring, for your information."

Harry's eyes were dark and unfathomable. He shrugged. "A jumping pony, then. Well, I've got this one. She's not a looker but she can jump all right."

They all crowded round the stable door and saw a small dun mare, with a caramel coat and black mane and tail, rolling her eyes and flattening back her ears.

"I don't think so," Mia said, hastily stepping back. "I need something a little bigger, I think – fourteen-two would be perfect."

Harry looked at Mia with narrow eyes then nodded, and they followed him to the next stable. Behind her back Mia was making wild waving movements with her hands. The others looked at each other blankly, following her a couple of steps behind.

"You all right?" Harry asked, and Mia pretended she was fanning her face because of the heat.

Charlie, who was always the first to crack whatever the situation, started to giggle and had to turn away from the others in case she caught Rosie's or Alice's eye and got set off properly.

"There's Popsicle here. He jumps like a cat."

"I'd rather one that jumped like a pony,"

Mia replied with a smile. Popsicle was chestnut.

"There's always Badger, I suppose," Harry said slowly.

"Badger?" Charlie repeated, swallowing her giggles in an instant. "I bet he's black and white, with a name like that."

"You're right, young lady," Harry replied with a lopsided smile. "He is."

They all crowded forward in a rush, but Badger was a heavy cob with a hogged mane and tail, nothing like the lighter-weight Moonlight. Rosie was unable to stop herself from sighing. Mia coughed loudly to cover it and asked if there were any more she could see. While Harry walked over to a stable at the far end of the yard, Mia hissed at the others to stop following her round like sheep and investigate the rest of the stables while she kept Harry occupied.

So, as she talked over the possibility of an undersized skewbald pony in the corner, Alice, Charlie and Rosie wandered round, dodging the skinny stable lad, who'd picked up a broom and started sweeping the yard. They looked over the other stable doors, trying to be casual, which was quite difficult with Growler following their every step, staring menacingly from underneath his shaggy eyebrows.

They weren't having any luck. Most of the ponies were cobby types, and Rosie fell in love with one sorrel pony, with a deep chestnut body and pale mane and tail. So far everything was looking above board… until Charlie whispered to Alice that she'd seen from up on the hill that there were more stables out the back of the main yard. But when they tried to nip round there to get a closer look, Harry suddenly turned sharply and with one shot of his bullet-black eyes stopped them dead in their tracks.

Mia clocked his reaction at once.

"Well," she said breezily, "you haven't really got anything round here that I like. Can I see the ones in the stables round the back?"

"Nothing round there that you'd be interested in," Harry said, in a voice that had turned to steel. Even Mia faltered in her step. In an instant she realised that there was something, or some pony, round in the back stables that Harry Franklin didn't want them to see.

"Can't be sure until I've been round there myself..." Mia persisted. They *had* to get a look.

But as Mia made a move forward, Harry took a step sideways and blocked her path.

"Like I said, nothing round there for you to be bothering with, young madam."

Mia half smiled.

"So, you *do* have more ponies round there then?" she asked sweetly.

Harry kept his stare level.

"I don't know exactly what you lot are after, but you're not going to find it on this yard. Got it?" he said quietly.

His face was like flint. His black eyes twitched. Charlie and Alice were nodding their heads, starting to back away, while Mia stared at Harry long and hard as she tried to battle him down with her fierceness. But she was fast learning that no one could out-fierce Harry Franklin and, seeing that standing there all day staring at each other would get her nowhere, Mia finally conceded defeat as graciously as possible.

"We may have been unlucky today, but I'll be keeping an eye on which ponies go in and which go out. That way I can spot a good one if it arrives," Mia said smoothly. "Or leaves."

"I think it's you who ought to be leaving. And if I see you hanging around here again..." Harry said menacingly, taking a step towards them. He let his threat sink in for a second as the girls gulped, then continued. "After all, it's obvious you're not serious about looking for a new pony."

"Oh, I am serious, Mr Franklin, it's just that I have a very specific pony in mind and I suspected he might be on your yard, that's all."

Mia might have been acting cool as she turned

away and walked briskly back to Wish, but her hands were shaking as she fumbled with her headcollar. Wish didn't help by nudging her for treats. She looked sideways and noticed that Alice and Rosie were having the same problem, but Charlie had Pirate free and was already mounted. Mia, Rosie and Alice weren't far behind. This time they left through the front entrance and Harry watched until they'd turned out onto the lane.

"He's hiding something – it *must* be Harry Franklin who stole Moonlight!" Mia said, looking scared but triumphant as they trotted the ponies quickly away from the yard. "Moonlight has to be hidden round the back. Why else would he behave so oddly about us going round there?"

They all started talking at once, except Alice. She looked down and patted her jodhpur pocket. Her heart sank. She pulled Scout up and called out to the others, who stopped.

"I've left my gloves in the yard – I must have

dropped them somehow." Alice wouldn't really have cared, but they were a present from her grandparents and she didn't want to lose them.

"We'll wait here then," Rosie said quickly, "but don't be long. I need to get back for my lunch – I'm in danger of fading away."

"Aren't you all coming with me?" Alice asked, looking round wildly. Her hands started to shake. Again.

"Someone has to hold the ponies," Mia pointed out.

"Isn't *anyone* going to come?" Alice said, looking at Charlie desperately.

"You'll be much quicker on your own," Charlie said, smiling sweetly.

Alice sighed, feeling abandoned as she dismounted and handed Scout's reins to Rosie. Friends indeed, she said to herself as she trudged back up the lane alone, trying to distract herself from how terrified she was feeling inside. Jumping in the Fratton Cup would be *nothing* compared to this, she thought, as she crept back into the yard on jelly-like legs.

Alice was in luck. The yard was silent except for the occasional stomp of a pony's hoof and the rhythmical munching of hay. And there were her gloves, still lying where she'd tied Scout. For half a second she wondered if she could just take a quick peep round the back. It was her chance to be a hero!

Then again, she didn't think her heart would stand it. Harry Franklin might be round there *right now* – she'd bump straight into him! No, just get the gloves and run, she told herself firmly. But as she reached down for them Alice heard Harry's muffled voice coming from inside his office. She tiptoed a step closer and listened in.

"You'll have to come and fetch him sooner."

Silence.

"I'll tell you why, because there've been people here sniffing around, *that's* why. I've got my hands on the pony you wanted and I've kept him well hidden, but I'm sure someone's got wind of what you're up to. I want this pony off my yard. I'm in the business of selling ponies, not being security and keeping nosey girls out. Got it?"

Alice held her breath, straining to hear the dealer's next response.

"Just come and get him as soon as possible, will you?"

Silence.

"Well, I suppose sometime after four today will have to be all right."

She heard the phone slam down and, grabbing her gloves tightly, she turned tail and sprinted out of the yard.

When she reached the others her chest was burning from running so fast.

"Where's the fire?" Rosie asked. Alice ignored her and all but vaulted into the saddle, fishing for her stirrups as she set off on a surprised Scout at a rapid trot along the lane, saying she'd tell them when they'd got further away.

They stopped when they saw a bridleway leading into a wood and found a shallow brook in the shade. They let the ponies have a drink, and a splash around, cooling their legs down as Alice told them in a single breath what she'd heard.

"I don't know who was on the other end of the phone but it *has* to be Moonlight in that stable, doesn't it?"

"And whoever Harry spoke to will be coming to collect him today," Mia said urgently, checking her watch.

Alice nodded.

"There's only one thing for it then," Mia announced solemnly. "We can't afford to miss the handover – we'll have to go back and do a stake-out."

Chapter Five

A shot of fear rushed through Alice at the thought of staking out hulking Harry Franklin's yard. Imagine if they got caught! Harry would probably feed them to Growler. Half of her was excited, the other half terrified. Either way, Alice was determined not to give up now that they were so close to solving the mystery, not when she was just starting to feel like a proper detective.

Rosie was looking less convinced.

"I'm not doing anything before we go back to the farm for some lunch," she said, pointedly breathing in to make herself look in need of a good meal. "All this talk of steaks is making me even hungrier than ever!"

"STAKE, not STEAK!" Charlie cried, tapping

Rosie's crash cap with her crop. "And anyway, if we go back to Blackberry Farm we might miss the handover – what if whoever's coming arrives early?! Then we won't have *any* way of finding out who took Moonlight."

Rosie twirled her whip, her lower lip jutting out.

"Think of Poppy – we're doing this for her," Alice said.

"I'd rather be doing something for my stomach right now, if you don't mind!" she snapped back. "And your plan won't work anyway. We couldn't hide last time with our ponies, remember. We'll have to go back to drop them off."

"Annoyingly, Rosie *has* got a point," Charlie said, looking frustrated.

"Again," Rosie said, a small smile of satisfaction spreading over her round face.

"I know!" Alice said, suddenly thinking of a way round the problem. "Daisy's house isn't far from here. We could see if she'd let us turn out our ponies in one of her fields, then we could come back on foot."

Three of them agreed, but Rosie still wouldn't budge.

"She might make us sandwiches," Alice said, trying to persuade her.

Alice also had her own reasons for this new plan. Daisy had a full set of show jumps that her father drilled her over endlessly in his efforts to transform Daisy from a slightly dippy rider into an international show jumper. Alice was hoping she could school Scout over them before turning him out.

So with Rosie grumbling loudly about how faint she felt, they set off in the direction of Daisy's. After ten minutes walking the ponies on long reins they reached Daisy's detached, isolated house. Alice jumped off and ran up the path to ring the doorbell. It echoed loudly inside. Empty. Alice walked round the side of the house and saw Daisy's black pony, Shadow, grazing alone.

He lifted his head when he saw Alice and flattened back his ears, shaking his head grumpily and flicking his tail before returning to graze. In the next field were the pristine show jumps, in a clearly marked-out arena. It was so tempting, but Alice knew they couldn't just ride round without asking, or unsaddle their ponies and turn them out without permission, especially knowing what Daisy's dad was like. He'd be furious if he found out that the 'competition' were using his jumps to improve their chances of winning the Cup and depriving Daisy.

For Rosie, finding no one at home was the last straw. She muttered, "I *knew* this was a bad idea!" before heading Dancer down the lane in the direction of home. Reluctantly, the others followed. There was nothing else they could do. They'd have to go back to Blackberry Farm after all.

At the end of the lane they walked and trotted quietly for a while through the woods feeling glum, when suddenly Daisy shot out of a side path, almost riding straight into them. She looked totally startled.

"Wow!" Charlie exclaimed as Pirate jinked sideways. "You don't hang around!"

"Wh— what do you mean...?" Daisy whispered, her eyes as big as saucers and her face looking a shade paler than normal.

"We rode past your place about twenty minutes ago," Alice explained, still thinking of the show jumps, "and it was deserted apart from Shadow. You must have got back and tacked up about a second after we called for you."

"Bad timing," Rosie sighed grumpily. "If only you'd turned up five minutes earlier we could have been enjoying a decent lunch by now."

Daisy looked alarmed. "You... you called at my house? What, for lunch...?"

"Not exactly. We were hoping we could turn out our ponies with Shadow for a while, that was all," Charlie replied, as Daisy hurriedly started to circle her pony away on the narrow path.

The girls exchanged looks. Daisy was often a bit on the loopy side, but she was behaving more bizarrely than usual even by her standards.

"Sorry," she replied hesitantly over her shoulder, not looking the others in the eye. "I'd ask you back now, only, well I know my dad wouldn't like it. He can be a bit funny about... erm..."

"Everything?" Rosie huffed.

Daisy nodded slightly. "Kind of."

Mia was about to push it, but Alice jumped in. "It's okay, Daisy, it was only a thought. Thanks anyway."

Daisy gave Alice a weak smile as she quickly walked Shadow away and disappeared down the path the girls had just ridden along.

"Is she going home already?" Charlie asked. "Shadow can only have been out for about ten minutes. That's hardly enough time to even warm him up."

"She's getting odder each time we see her," Mia said.

"It's really not her fault," Alice replied, defensively. "*She's* all right – I bet it's her ridiculously strict dad piling on the pressure this close to the Show."

"Well, he can't be that strict or he'd make sure she groomed that poor pony properly," Mia sniffed. "He looks dreadful. I'd never turn Wish out looking like that, even for a hack."

Charlie, Alice and Rosie smiled at one another. Mia often said the same thing about their ponies, especially Pirate, whose bushy black mane defied gravity no matter what Charlie tried. No one lived up to Mia's high turnout standards, and if she was annoyed with someone, being superior about their grooming was Mia's favourite put-down.

"Looks like we'll have to go back home after all," Rosie said. She tried and failed to keep the triumph out of her voice.

U U U U

Once they reached Blackberry Farm the girls
turned out the ponies as soon as they'd drunk
some water and had their backs and legs hosed
down. Scout got down straight away and rolled
happily and Dancer copied him, grunting loudly
as she kicked her legs in the air and almost got
stuck on her broad back.

Alice drank some water from the hose on the
yard, and when Charlie tried to take it the hose
flipped, accidentally, on Mia, who shrieked as
if someone was trying to kill her. Before Alice
could stop her, Mia had grabbed the hosepipe to
exact her revenge and after a couple of well-aimed
blasts they were all sopping wet. Even Rosie, as
she emerged from the tack room with her packed
lunch in her hand, got a blast full in the face.

"Mind my sandwiches!" she shrieked, holding
them above her head.

The girls sat on the paddock fence in the sun

to dry off, hungrily eating the lunches they'd brought with them from home. The ponies all wandered over to them, with Dancer stretching out her neck and nibbling Rosie's knee until she gave in and shared her sandwich with her. After they'd finished, Mia checked her watch and flipped open her notebook again. Looking down the clues, they felt pleased with what they'd found out so far.

"I can almost taste victory!" Rosie announced.

"What, even through cheese and pickle?" asked Charlie.

Mia coughed. "Listen, we haven't got long to go through this before we have to head back to Harry's – we need to concentrate."

Rosie saluted Mia, making Charlie and Alice giggle as they all turned their attention back to the notebook:

Clue 1
Solid metal gate, standard. New padlocks

on there – maybe put on since the theft
of Moonlight?

Clue 2
No tack was stolen with Moonlight.

Clue 3
~~Tracks on the pa...~~
Tracks on the path – hooves only – whoever
took Moonlight must have led him away
from the yard on foot to begin with because
there was no way they could load him into
a trailer or horsebox without being heard.

Clue 4
Person who stole Moonlight _must_ be local to
know about him and how to get him away
from Hawthorn Farm.

Clue 5
Could be a local dealer – stealing to order?!

Clue 6
Harry Franklin - dealer who has a yard
close to Hawthorn Farm.

Clue 7
After inspection of his yard, Harry Franklin
has a pony (<u>Moonlight?</u>) which he wants to
keep hidden.

Clue 8
Phone call - Harry arranging for someone
to come and collect the pony that they've
made him keep hidden.

They sat back, satisfied.

"There's no point getting settled, everyone," Mia said, turning the page on her notebook to reveal the following:

Action Point 1
Stake out Harry Franklin's yard to watch for

*mystery person collecting mystery pony
(Moonlight?).*

*Action Point 2
Get photo of pony (Moonlight) as he is
picked up from Harry Franklin's yard, to use
as hard evidence.*

"We've got to go back there without any further delay," Mia announced, jumping down from the fence.

"Has anyone actually thought about *how* we're going to get there? There's no way I'm walking that far!" Rosie complained. "And we can't take the ponies out again – they've done enough today already and they'd be a bit of a giveaway, anyway, unless we teach them all to hide under that big bush."

"We could cycle," Charlie suggested. "It's only two now, so we could be there by three at the latest."

"Great – my bike's got a puncture, I can't go,"

Rosie huffed but was secretly pleased. She didn't like the idea of cycling so far in the blazing summer heat one little bit.

"We could take it in turns to double up?" Alice offered.

"I hardly think so. You don't want to be carrying around a lump like me," Rosie said, puffing herself out to make herself look as big as possible.

"Well, if you're staying you won't mind me asking if I can borrow your brother's bike, seeing as I haven't got my own here," Mia said, pleased that she'd thought of it first – Rosie's brother Will had a *really* good bike. "But if you don't come, Rosie, and we find Moonlight, you lose your share of any reward."

Rosie narrowed her eyes. "But I got the clue about the hoof prints."

"Look, come or don't come. Either way, we have to get going. And I think we should call our parents to let them know we'll be late home." Mia got up briskly, reaching for her mobile.

Charlie and Alice followed. Alice turned to see Rosie sitting moodily on the fence still, gently pulling Dancer's ears, and thought for a second that she really was bailing out. But as they turned the corner Rosie suddenly jumped down and ran to catch up. When she saw Alice and Charlie smiling to themselves, she dropped back to a grumpy walk.

Fifteen minutes later they were ready to leave the yard. Mia had found Will out in one of the fields checking on the sheep. He'd cheerfully headed back to the yard and wheeled out his huge red bike for her, and Rosie had reluctantly agreed to take it in turns to double up with the others.

Alice was first to cycle with Rosie as it had been her suggestion. Rosie sat on the saddle and steered while Alice held the handle bars and pedalled standing up. After about a quarter of a mile Alice was exhausted and Rosie swapped onto Charlie's bike, but Charlie couldn't manage to pedal hard enough to keep her small bike going with Rosie sitting on it. Rosie stomped over to Mia, who could only just reach the pedals on Will's bike.

Mia panicked after three minutes, braking violently, and claiming that she swore she heard the main shaft crack. None of the rest of them knew what a 'main shaft' was but it sounded important and Mia convinced them it was serious. So Rosie got shunted back to Alice and they muddled along, with Rosie moaning in Alice's ear every five seconds that she couldn't see to steer. Alice thought at first she was just being awkward until they wobbled headlong into a bramble bush.

With lots of pit stops, filled with Rosie complaining about the cycling making her ravenous, it took them longer than they thought to reach the edge of Harry Franklin's paddocks. They walked the bikes up to the top of the slope where they'd hidden earlier that morning and pushed them roughly into the hedge, keeping them nearby in case they had to make a quick getaway.

"What do we do now?" Rosie asked, collapsing dramatically and lying flat out on the grass in the sun.

"We sit and wait until we see a horsebox approaching, then we sneak down and get a photograph as they load Moonlight. Then we phone the police," Mia announced. "Simple."

So they sat down on the warm grass behind the hedge and waited.

And waited.

Rosie let out an occasional slight snore as Alice made endless daisy chains and Charlie saw how much grass she could put in Rosie's hair before she noticed. Suddenly Mia peered over at the yard and squeaked. The others looked up, with Rosie wondering where she was for a second, as Mia pointed silently.

Lying on their fronts, they peeped through the hedge and saw Harry walk out into the yard. Somehow he looked even larger than before, and Alice felt a shiver go down her spine despite the warm summer sun. Harry had his big grey lurcher loping along by his side. It looked as if Harry was taking Growler out for a walk.

Rosie groaned. "We could be here all night at this rate!"

Charlie stood up, stooping to keep hidden by the hedge. "Look, rather than hanging about up here, which isn't getting us anywhere, why don't we sneak down to the yard now while Harry's out, get a photo of Moonlight, then make a run for it."

"What, go down there now? Before the handover?" Alice gasped. "But he'll go mad if he finds us on his yard. You heard what he said about us ever coming back here!"

"He won't even know we've been," Charlie said. "We'll be in and out before he has a chance to see us."

Alice looked seriously doubtful.

"You can always stay here by yourself all night if you'd prefer," Charlie called back to them as she scrambled over the hedge and darted off down the hill to the yard. Filled with excitement and nerves, Alice jumped up and followed her, snagging her jods on the way over. Alice heard a cry and guessed Rosie had done the same, but she didn't turn to check. By the time Alice reached the stables her heart was racing. She told herself that it must have been the running.

Charlie motioned for them all to head straight across the main yard and round to the stables at the back. It was a huge risk, heading in the same direction that Harry had disappeared in, but they had no choice. Alice was two steps behind Charlie, and she heard Mia's voice in her ear hissing at Rosie to stop pulling at her T-shirt or it would lose its shape. Charlie edged slowly round the corner then suddenly stopped dead and whipped back. Alice crashed into her, Mia into Alice, and Rosie collapsed, panting, on all of them, almost knocking them to the floor in a heap. The look on Charlie's face said all they needed to know: Harry Franklin was on his way back... with Growler!

They turned quickly back into the main yard. Suddenly they saw the office door opposite where they were standing start to open. The skinny stable lad! They'd all totally forgotten about him! Alice, Rosie and Charlie panicked – they were trapped, with Harry advancing in one direction, the skinny lad in the other! There was no way they'd make it out of the yard without being seen now! Without thinking, Mia quickly scraped back the bolt on the nearest stable door and bundled the others inside. She swung the door shut and scraped the top bolt across, ducking down behind the door just as footsteps stepped out across the yard from the office. Mia stayed stock still for a second. Then, still bent double, she turned to make her way to the back of the stable where the others were hiding. She came nose to nose with a huge white horse – Harry's huge white horse. The horse snorted. Even his nostrils were vast. He stomped his hoof, and as Mia glanced down she noticed that his hoofs were also seriously huge. With a gulp, she edged round him and joined the others who had shoved themselves as tightly as possible into the furthest, gloomiest corner.

The massive horse shifted his back legs round, turning so that he was facing them. He lowered his head and snuffled them. Rosie tried to squeeze further behind Charlie, who was trying to inch behind Alice. Alice, cramped in the corner on her heels, felt herself tipping forward and pushed back on them both. As Rosie opened her mouth to protest Mia shot her a warning glance, holding a finger to her lips with one hand and trying to push the huge, inquisitive, whiskery white muzzle away with the other.

There was a light patter of feet outside. Alice tried to breathe so silently that she started to feel faint. A dog's nose snuffled outside, his shadow just visible as it broke up the crack of sunshine under the stable door.

Then the metallic ring of steel-toecapped boots clopped closer.

"All right, boss?" The girls hadn't heard the skinny worker talk before, but they figured it must be him. Harry grunted in reply then stopped outside the big white horse's stable.

"What's wrong, Colossus?" Harry asked. The horse, unsettled, stepped forward to the front of the stable and nodded his massive head up and down. Alice was convinced that her heart was beating so loudly Harry would be able to hear it from where he was standing. The four girls were cramped in the corner, squished into the straw. Alice's legs were starting to burn but she didn't dare move an inch.

Suddenly Rosie's stomach let out an almighty rumble, echoing round the stable. The girls' mouths dropped open as they stared at Rosie, whose eyes nearly popped out of her head.

"What's that?" Harry boomed. The girls leaned back into the shadows even further, starting to shake as they glared at Rosie, certain she'd just given them away. "Are you hungry, Colossus, is that it?"

As the footsteps disappeared for a second the others let out a collective, shaky sigh.

"What? I *warned* you I was hungry!" Rosie mouthed, as Charlie nudged her.

Suddenly, a slice of hay was lumped over the door. Harry loitered outside.

"Who forgot to put the bottom bolt on your stable, eh, Colossus? Better go in and check that nothing's amiss. Isn't that right, Growler? Yes, isn't that right?" Harry said in a surprisingly high, soppy voice, patting the dog loudly.

A bolt was slowly scraped back and the lower stable door opened an inch. A crack of sunshine appeared, along with a long, furry snout.

At the same second a mobile phone rang out, shattering the silence. Rosie went pale – it was her ring tone! It was her phone! She must have forgotten to turn it off, she thought, scrabbling for it in her pocket and elbowing Alice in the nose. This was it – she'd led the others into the shaggy grey jaws of doom!

"Where are you? On your way?" Harry barked, at the same moment that Rosie's hand closed round her own phone. The screen was blank. With her heart galloping she let out a long, silent sigh and sank back into the straw, squashing the others even more as they silently protested with shoves and glares. Rosie was about to slide her mobile back into her pocket when she looked up and saw the door was still open an inch. The big snout was still there. Rosie shivered as the snout edged the door open an inch more. One black, glinting eye looked round, then fixed itself upon her. But the next second Harry, his mobile still stuck to his ear, used his large boot to hook Growler back from the door.

"I'll get the pony ready," Harry said. "Now, about payment..."

He swung the stable door shut, slid the top bolt then kicked the bottom lock across. The rest of the conversation was lost as he stomped out of earshot.

Mia, huddled in the corner behind the others, looked stricken.

"He's shut the bottom bolt!" she whispered. "We're trapped!"

Chapter
Six

"WE might be trapped," Charlie whispered, feeling hot and sticky from crouching awkwardly in the corner, "but at least we haven't been caught."

"That was close, though!" Rosie said, puffing out her pink cheeks as she fanned her face with her hand.

Her insides felt upside down and she was secretly glad that she was sitting and not having to run anywhere or be heroic at that precise moment.

"Listen!" Mia hissed quietly, holding her hand in the air.

They all fell silent. The huge white horse, Colossus, stopped munching for a second, too, raising his head and taking a massive step up to the door, his big ears pricked forward. It was getting louder by the second – the unmistakable drone of a horsebox, gears changing down then revving as it slowed for the turning into the drive, then accelerating up the drive and braking in the yard with a hiss.

"They're here," Mia mouthed and took a deep breath. They all looked at one another, feeling nervousness and excitement bubble through them.

Alice felt her knees give and she grabbed hold of Rosie, who nearly jumped out of her skin, making Charlie start to giggle nervously before gulping and biting her lip to keep silent. Horsebox doors were slammed and a couple of people jumped down onto concrete. The girls crept nearer to the stable door, avoiding Colossus's flashing tail, and straining to hear snippets of conversation as Harry clacked over to meet whoever had just arrived in the driveway. Three sets of footsteps walked into the yard, stopping not far from the grey horse's stable. Alice felt a bead of sweat trickle down between her shoulder blades as she heard the voices – they were just the other side of the wooden stable wall!

"So, you managed to get your hands on the pony my son here had his eye on," a deep voice boomed. "No trouble keeping everything hush-hush at this end?"

"It was easy keeping everything under wraps to begin with," Harry replied, "until today when some girls came round, one with a proper-looking show pony."

In spite of the situation, Mia allowed herself a small, superior smile.

"They kept mentioning the Fratton Show and trying to get round to these stables where I've hidden your pony. I think they knew more than they let on, but I put them off. Just," Harry explained.

"Good. That's what you're being paid extra for, to keep this 'special' deal quiet, remember?" the deep voice replied coldly.

As the other girls looked at each other with widening eyes, Mia eased her notebook out of her pocket. She began quietly scribbling their conversation down, collecting the evidence.

"Come on, Dad, I don't want to hang around here all day," a new, younger male voice piped up. "Can't we just get the pony and load him up?"

The girls' jaws dropped. They glanced at one another, their eyes wide with disbelief. The voice was unmistakable. Mia wrote down a name in capital letters, then tapped the notebook. The others read, then nodded their heads vigorously.

MARK TICKLE!

But they couldn't be shocked for long. Mia would only have a second to get a photo on her mobile phone of Moonlight as he was led through the yard to the waiting horsebox. She switched her mobile to camera mode. Alice pointed out silently that she needed to turn off the flash option.

Mia stepped lightly and hunkered down beneath the half door in the shadows, her hands shaking as she held the phone.

The hoof beats got louder as they passed right by Colossus's stable. Mia waited for as long as she dared, then as the hoof beats tripped away she popped her hand over the stable door while staying well hidden and took a picture.

She scooted back and they all huddled round to see the result. It wasn't easy to see in the gloom of the stable and it was a bit blurry because Mia's hand had been shaking. She'd taken it at an angle, and most of what was visible of the pony was covered in a huge, lightweight summer rug. Mia looked disappointed for a second, then saw, in among the muddle of human legs, a pony's back leg. It was an off hind. And it was white. They all peered closely in turn at the photo of Moonlight stuck into Mia's notebook from the 'Missing' advert. It showed that his near hind was black, from his stifle to his hoof. But the off hind, his right back leg which Mia had just caught on camera, was all white.

"It's him!" Charlie whispered urgently, peering at the phone. "It's Moonlight!"

"Shh!" Alice hissed. "They're still talking!"

They strained their ears again. Then the horse-box roared into life.

"Good luck at the Fratton Show," Harry shouted over the engine noise. "He better win after all this effort."

"Oh, there's no question about him being placed first. This one's a proven winner. There'll be no disguising *that* bit once we get there! All this will be worth it then, as Mark here picks up the red rosette," Mark's dad replied. The horsebox rolled down the drive and rumbled away into the early evening.

The girls sank back in the straw, exhausted and elated at the same time. But as Rosie did a victory shuffle she spooked Colossus. Unsettled already by their presence and all the activity on the yard, he began to pace his stable. They all rushed to get out of his path and squeezed against the back wall, breathing silently, as Harry returned to the main yard, rustling something in his hands.

"Easy money, Growler, easy money. Come on, boy – I don't know why you've decided to guard Colossus's box tonight." He stopped and called the dog again. Growler whined and scratched at the stable door.

"What's in there, Growler?"

Alice stopped breathing.

"Are there rats? Shall we open the door for you to get the rats? Shall we?"

Alice froze. She stole a glance at the others; they all looked exactly how she felt – petrified and in a state of total panic.

"Too late now, Growler old boy. The rats can live until tomorrow."

The girls let out a collective long, silent breath.

But outside Growler still refused to shift. If he didn't disappear they'd never be able to escape without his alerting Harry. Harry hovered nearby, trying to coax the reluctant Growler away, while Colossus circled his box again. As they huddled in the corner, Colossus let out a loud, body-shaking neigh, which pierced the girls' ears as they stood just behind him. Harry stomped over. Already stiff and uncomfortable, the girls squeezed as tightly as they could into the shadows, desperate not to get caught and have to face the wrath of Harry. If he discovered them now, he'd know they'd just witnessed him selling a stolen pony to Mark Tickle. And if he was mad at them earlier just for sniffing around the yard, who could tell how furious he'd get for this? The girls clung together. Rosie closed her eyes and crossed her legs, suddenly feeling desperate for a wee.

At that precise moment Colossus lifted his tail. A strong smell preceded the droppings that followed the tail lifting, but in his excitement they shot out further than normal. Much further. Charlie and Alice silently ducked either side of the long grey tail. Rosie, left crouching between them, still had her eyes tight shut. There wasn't the usual bounce on straw as the droppings landed, because they didn't land on straw. Rosie's eyes popped open. Mia just got her hand over Rosie's mouth in time, covering it fiercely as Rosie threatened to squeal.

Harry patted Colossus's big neck. "Calm down, old boy. Come on, Growler. Dinner time."

Finally the big lurcher turned and followed his master at the mention of dinner, his claws tippy-tapping across the yard. Charlie and Alice doubled over, collapsing into the straw in fits of silent giggles as Rosie at last removed Mia's hand from her mouth.

"This is not funny!" she hissed dramatically. She moaned quietly as she looked at the droppings that had dribbled down her.

While Rosie attempted to use some straw to wipe her T-shirt, she glanced up at Charlie and Alice who were weak from trying to stifle their laughter. Rosie bit her lip, trying to keep up her look of disgust until she saw Mia wiping away a tear, her face crinkling as she tried to control herself. Suddenly Mia's laugh escaped as a snort and she waved her hand around, cracking up again, and Rosie finally dissolved into giggles too.

After being silent and still for so long, and with Harry safely out of the way, they all felt hysterical and for a minute none of them could move. After sitting cramped up for ages, and suddenly exhausted after the all the tension had drained from her, Alice stood up and slowly stretched her achy legs. She had to turn away from Rosie to keep herself under control as the others started to unfold themselves too. Finally, when they were all standing up, they crept to the front of the stable, patting Colossus. The big grey had calmed down and he breathed warmly over them, snuffling across Alice's hair.

"So, what do we do now?" she asked quietly. "About Moonlight, I mean?"

"First things first," Charlie said, looking over the stable door. "We need to get out of here. Coast's clear. Someone give me a leg-up?"

Mia and Alice cupped their hands together, and when Charlie put her knee in they hauled her up, then she leaped down the other side, landing as quietly as possible, and quickly pulled back the bolts. Alice locked them after they'd all silently slunk out. Then they scooted across the yard and up the hill, bending low, until they reached the hedge with the bikes in it. Hauling them out, they jumped on and pedalled manically back to Blackberry Farm.

"Can you believe it was Mark Tickle?" Alice asked, desperately trying to distract herself from the back-breaking pedalling on her bike which only had one gear, and the overpowering smell of horse dung wafting up from Rosie's clothes. "I mean, I knew he was competitive, but stealing the top pony to secure a win? That's just madness."

"It's more than madness," Charlie replied.

"It's total craziness. He can't possibly think that he can turn up to the Fratton Show and ride Moonlight in the Cup. Everyone would recognise the piebald immediately, especially Poppy – he'd be mobbed! His plan would backfire before he'd even had a chance to jump the first fence."

"Charlie has a serious point," Rosie puffed.

"So why, exactly, did he go to the lengths of stealing a pony he'd never get away with competing on in the Cup?" Mia asked.

Everyone fell into a thoughtful silence. After being so close to solving the case, they now felt as if it was crumbling around them. It just didn't make sense. Mia braked abruptly, resting Will's bike against her leg. She pulled out and flipped open her notebook, reading it back to herself. Suddenly her face lit up.

"It's here!" she squealed, pointing at her neat scribbles from the overheard snippets of conversation in the stable. "Mark's dad gave us the clue himself!"

They all crowded round as she continued.

"He said there'd be no *disguising* Moonlight's talent. That can only mean one thing, can't it?"

"What exactly?" Rosie asked, not quite following.

"Well, if he can't disguise the *talent*, he'll have to disguise the *pony*!" Mia cried.

"How will he do that?" Alice asked, getting off the bike with Rosie and collapsing on the grass verge for a proper breather. The others joined her and they became lost in thought as the warm evening sky turned dusky pink.

"Boot polish?" Charlie finally suggested. "Something like that maybe?"

"Yuk! Poor Moonlight!" Rosie exclaimed. "So, what are we going to do about it?"

"We need to come up with a plan to expose Mark at the show, right in front of all the crowds. And Poppy," Mia said thoughtfully.

"Only not this evening," Rosie said with a huge yawn.

Now they'd worked out the hard part of who had stolen Moonlight and why, the next step would have to wait until they'd all had a good night's sleep. Wearily, but with a glow of triumph as warm as the sinking sun, they picked up the bikes and started to pedal the rest of the way back to Blackberry Farm.

Chapter Seven

As much as Alice enjoyed doing lots of detective work, she was secretly relieved the next morning that she was free to do her own thing for a bit. The Fratton Show was drawing ever closer and she still hadn't schooled Scout. She'd got up extra early to go to Blackberry Farm. Charlie had said she'd do the same, only she overslept, and leaned out of her bedroom window to tell Alice she'd catch her up.

Scout was waiting for Alice as always by the paddock fence and whickered softly as she cycled into the yard. The other ponies wandered over to the gate, and Alice slipped on Scout's and Wish's headcollars and led them both in before heading back for Pirate and Dancer. After she'd put them in their stables she quickly mixed their small feeds while Dancer kicked her stable door demandingly, the deep whicker getting louder and louder as Rosie appeared sleepily from the farm door and carried over her feed bucket.

After the ponies had finished eating, Rosie and Alice tied Dancer and Scout up outside their stables in the cool, early morning sun. While Rosie faffed about sorting through her grooming kit, Alice gave Scout a thorough brushing until his dappled grey coat shone. Scout nibbled and pulled at his haynet and every now and again he turned his head, watching Alice with his soft, friendly dark eyes. He stood solidly while she brushed all around his legs, and as she lightly pulled his feathers, he lifted each hoof in turn for her to pick out.

Then she decided to tidy his mane, backcombing it and gently pulling out the longer strands until it was shorter and all the same length, making it easier to plait. Scout held his head low, so that she could reach all the way up to his ears, his eyes half closed and his lower lip drooping.

Once she'd finished and was happy with his neatly hanging mane (apart from the bit by his ears, where she'd got carried away and it was sticking upright), Scout nudged her arm and she found a carrot for him in her pocket. He lifted one front hoof and waved it as she held the carrot out to him. His soft lips hoovered it up, and he crunched noisily and happily while she went to fetch his tack.

Mia and Charlie had arrived at the yard by then, and they joined Alice and Rosie as they headed to the well-worn track in the small schooling paddock. After they had worked the ponies in, Alice turned Scout towards one of the pairs of faded wooden jump wings with the flaking cross poles that was set up in the middle of the paddock. Scout felt confident and strong in Alice's hands going into the fence. She softened her reins as they got to it and he cleared it easily.

While Mia walked Wish to one side ("I'll judge your jumping," she'd announced to the others before turning her face towards the sun and closing her eyes), the rest of them slid off their ponies and mapped out a course as they hauled their collection of rickety poles and barrels about the field, building an upright, spread and double before taking it in turns to jump round. Pirate went first and flew each fence, rattling them but somehow leaving them all standing.

Next up was Dancer, who approached each fence at a snail's pace, eyeing them suspiciously even though she'd seen them a hundred times before. Nothing Rosie did could make her go any faster. She slowed on the way to the first fence, then launched herself over. Rosie collapsed on her neck, giggling and heading vaguely for the next jump.

Despite Charlie and Alice yelling "Legs!" at the top of their voices, Rosie was still giggling too much to use them effectively. Dancer cat-leaped the next fence then ground to a halt in front of the third. Rosie sank in the saddle dramatically. While Alice and Charlie groaned, Rosie just shook her head.

"It's not my fault – Dancer just isn't built to jump." She shrugged good-humouredly, joining Mia and letting her reins go to the buckle end. Dancer dropped her head immediately with a snort before ravenously starting to crop the patchy grass in the dusty field.

As Mia rolled up her short sleeves to get a better tan, Alice set off around the course. Scout bounded into canter from walk and bounced forward over the dry summer grass, picking up neatly at each fence and jumping carefully, his ears pricked as he kept looking for the next one. Maybe all their hacking had freshened him up, Alice thought happily as they soared clean over the small triple bar.

"And the winner of the Blackberry Farm Cup

is Alice Hathaway riding Scout!" Rosie joked through coned hands.

Alice laughed as Scout put in a series of high-spirited bucks. If only, she wished for the hundredth time, she could feel as relaxed in the show ring as she did in the field.

"Then, Scout," she whispered as her pony's grey ear flickered back and forward at the sound of her voice, "we might have a chance in the real thing, I'm sure of it!"

U U U U

Over the next couple of days they concentrated on getting ready for the show. Mia spent hours on Wish's appearance and practising her show-ring routine. Wish walked, trotted and cantered neatly in figures of eight with her neck arched gracefully. Her extended trot was a show-stopper and Mia practised that most of all, although she knew that Wish saved her best for when she had an audience. The sound of the crowd 'ooh'-ing in awe as the palomino mare flashed across the centre of the ring with a combination of power and elegance, her hoofs flicking out magnificently, elevated her to another level. Mia leaned down and hugged Wish. She'd worked hard to get her spot on, but she knew how lucky she was to have found a pony as talented as Wish, one that loved showing off to the crowd and the judge as much as she did. Charlie did nothing different from normal, just sat quietly and effortlessly as Pirate spun and bucked and charged about the schooling ring, while Rosie tried and failed to persuade Dancer to leave the ground from any pace other than a virtual standstill.

Alice schooled Scout on the flat and over some show jumps, and he was accurate, fast and responsive. Alice felt completely in tune with him and she was enjoying every second. She knew that jumping was his favourite thing, and since she'd got him it had become hers too.

"It's just your nerves that stop you, Alice," Charlie announced after they'd turned out their ponies in the warm, late afternoon sun, "I reckon it must be all those millions of eyes on you once you get in the ring that does it."

"Thanks for the reminder," Alice groaned.

As they wandered back to the yard they talked half about the classes they were entering and half about Moonlight. There was only one more day before the show, which was being held on the Sunday, and they still hadn't come up with a plan of action over how to confront Mark. Panic was starting to set in.

"We've got so much preparation to get through tomorrow with the ponies and the tack that we're not going to have a spare second!" Rosie whined, at the idea of all the work she needed to do the next day as much as anything else.

"But we can't just leave it to chance on Sunday morning once we get to the show," Charlie said.

"No way," Alice added, trying hard not to

think about how ill she'd be feeling on the day. "I'll be such a bag of nerves by then I won't be able to think straight so we'll have to get it sorted out before then."

"There's only one thing for it," Mia announced. "Rosie, if you agree, we'll have to have a sleepover tomorrow night."

Chapter Eight

Mia, Charlie and Alice arrived at Blackberry Farm the next morning with their overnight bags and show kits, bubbling over with excitement about spending the night there. Rosie's bedroom looked out across the paddocks, so they would be able to check on the ponies by the luminous light of the moon and the stars as they made their plans.

After they'd bundled their bags in the cottage and hung up their clothes, they raced back to the stables and concentrated on getting ready for the following day. The yard was soon awash with suds as the girls tied their ponies outside their stables and shampooed them, getting drenched as the ponies whirled their tails round after they'd been rinsed. They used a sweat scraper to squeakily squeeze off all the excess water from their ponies' coats.

After washing Pirate's tail, Charlie put a tail bandage on to try to make the hairs at the top lie flat, rather than spiking out like a huge hedgehog. Then the girls led their ponies to a patch of grass to crop while they dried off in the sun, with Dancer getting behind Rosie and nudging her along each step so that they could get there faster. Every now and again Scout stopped eating, and while Alice stroked his velveteen muzzle, prickly with whiskers, he rested his chin lightly on her shoulder, blinking his eyes.

Once Scout was turned out wearing his light summer sheet to keep him as clean as possible, Alice headed into the depths of the gloomy tack room, filled with its familiar strong smell of leather and saddle soap. Finding a sponge, she started cleaning her tack, scrubbing Scout's bit and all the metal buckles. She polished the leather on her saddle until it shone.

"Alice, you do realise that if you carry on like that you'll make the seat so slippery", Charlie pointed out, "that you'll slide off it after just one jump!"

This sent Alice into another spasm of nerves, but although they all offered various opinions, no one actually knew how to scuff up the leather once it had been polished so Alice just added it to the list of things to worry about the next day.

After they'd finished tack-cleaning and had given the ponies their small evening feed Alice gave Scout strict instructions not to get any grass stains on his beautifully clean and sparkling grey coat.

They yanked off their jodhpur boots, leaving piles of straw that fell out of them by the mat before running through the open back door of the farmhouse, into the large, cluttered kitchen. The smell of warm, fresh bread filled their noses. They scraped out the chairs and flopped at the big, scarred wooden kitchen table moaning about their aching arms after all that tack-cleaning as they cut huge chunks of the bread and buttered it haphazardly.

Rosie's mum, dressed in paint-spattered overalls, her messy blonde hair tied back with a long, dangling rainbow-coloured scarf, wandered in and poured them some lemonade.

"Home made," she announced proudly as she poured it, not noticing the girls grimacing as they took great gulps.

"Mum!" Rosie groaned. "I think you forgot to put any sugar in!"

Mrs Honeycott scratched her head with the small paintbrush she'd had tucked behind her ear.

"Did I?" she asked vaguely. "I must have been distracted."

"I think you're permanently distracted," Rosie muttered as the other girls giggled between mouthfuls of bread.

"What was that, sweetheart?" Mrs Honeycott asked as she piled salad onto plates and placed them on the table.

"Nothing," Rosie replied sweetly, before clocking the plates and frowning. "Er, haven't you forgotten something else, Mum?"

Rosie started to sniff the air, then they all noticed smoke drifting from the ancient aga. Mr Honeycott appeared at the back door at the same moment and pulled off his wellies, shaking his head.

"You go and finish your painting," he said, smiling broadly. "She's always like this when she's in the middle of a big project – you get used to it! I'll dish up."

Mrs Honeycott drifted off in the direction of her studio and Mr Honeycott rescued from the Aga the slightly burnt home-made pizza, piled high with fresh roasted vegetables that he'd grown. As he cut it into slices Beanie's beady eyes watched his every move, hoping for a scrap to fall. Beanie positioned himself by Rosie, head on one side, as she and the others tucked in, talking through mouthfuls about the show. Will, Rosie's older brother, rushed in, grabbed a slice of pizza then sat with Mr Honeycott discussing a problem with one of their tractors.

As soon as they'd finished the girls rushed up to Rosie's bedroom and plumped down on the air beds that Rosie had blown up and piled with sleeping bags and pillows. The walls were covered with sketches and paintings that Mrs Honeycott had made of Dancer, and every available surface was covered with framed photos of Rosie's strawberry roan mare. Rosie stroked the one by her bed, a close-up of Dancer's broad, honest cobby chestnut face with its white blaze, before collapsing on her bed. She pulled out a tin from under it, filled with all sorts of sweets.

"I got them for our midnight feast," she explained, chomping on some marshmallows and handing the tin round, "but there's no way I'm going to be able to stay awake till then so we might as well eat them now."

"You eat louder than Dancer!" Charlie joked

before Rosie swung her pillow, laughing as it missed Charlie and clocked Alice on the side of her head. Charlie and Alice both started to retaliate before Mia coughed pointedly, calling them to order, just as the bedroom door was butted open and Pumpkin the ginger cat strolled in.

"Right," Mia began, opening her notebook as the others stopped giggling and started to concentrate. They all studied the new clues:

Clue 9
Mystery person turns up at Harry Franklin's to collect mystery pony (Moonlight).

Clue 10
Harry Franklin and the buyer discuss underhand goings-on.

Clue 11
Mystery person turns out to be Mark Tickle!!

Clue 12
Photo of white near hind. <u>Matches</u>
<u>Moonlight's near hind!!</u>

Clue 13
Mark has got this pony (Moonlight) to make
sure he'll win at the Fratton Show!!!

Clue 14
Mark's dad says the pony in question is a
proven winner.

Clue 15 - KEY CLUE
Mark's dad mentions that he won't be able
to disguise the pony being a winner.
Meaning? <u>That he will be able to disguise</u>
<u>the pony itself!!</u>

Impressive, even if Mia had to say it herself. She hadn't missed one single tiny detail as she'd scribbled away in Colossus's gloomy stable.

"So," Alice asked, wishing for the hundredth time that she could be just a teeny bit more like Mia, "what should we do at the show tomorrow?"

"Let's just tell Mark as soon as he gets there that we know all about his plan and that it would be better for him to hand Moonlight over without any fuss," Charlie suggested. "That'll save lots of messing about."

"But if we do that he might just keep Moonlight hidden in the lorry and drive straight off," Mia said. "Then we won't have the chance to catch him out."

"Well, we all heard Mark's dad as good as admitting when he was at Harry Franklin's yard that he was planning to disguise Moonlight," Alice replied. "If Mark's going to use some kind of boot polish or dye to cover up the white bits, we need to figure out how we can get close enough to rub some of it off and prove in front of everyone that he's a thief."

"I've got it!" Charlie shouted as she jumped

up, almost dislodging Pumpkin, who was curled at the end of Rosie's bed. "We throw a bucket of soapy water over Moonlight as soon as Mark leads him out of the horsebox!"

"That sounds way too messy…" Mia began, making a face, "although… maybe, just *maybe* that could work."

"Bagsy I throw the water!" Rosie squealed, shooting her hand up in the air.

"Ok," Alice said, checking she'd got it right. "We confront Mark about Moonlight, and if he *doesn't* confess but denies it then Rosie throws water – *gently* – over Moonlight…"

"… and all is revealed!" Rosie beamed, stroking Pumpkin as his contented purrs rumbled all round the room. "Well, maybe all will be revealed with water followed by a bit of scrubbing, anyway."

"Right," Mia agreed, "and I'm sure Poppy will still come to the show, even without Moonlight. She'll want to see everyone and maybe ask around to see if anyone's got any news of him. So I think we should do this: one person collects Poppy and comes up with a reason for her to come over to Mark's horsebox. One person holds the ponies and acts as look-out…"

"Me! If I can't throw the water, I want to be lookout!" Charlie interrupted.

Mia made a note before carrying on: "… One person confronts Mark, and Rosie throws the water."

"What happens if he confesses before we throw the water?" Alice asked, even though that seemed highly unlikely. "We won't have to throw it if he does that."

"How will I know, though?" Rosie asked, sounding disappointed. "Maybe I should throw it anyway, just to be sure."

"No, Alice is right," Mia said, chewing her pencil. "We need a code word. Rosie, you can hide around the other side of Mark's horsebox. I'll confront him and if he confesses everything, forget the bucket. But if he isn't playing along, and you hear me shout 'CHEAT', that's your cue to throw it."

"So if Charlie's the lookout, Rosie is throwing the water and you're talking to Mark, I guess that leaves me with the job of collecting Poppy," Alice said, slightly grumpily. After all, it was the least glamorous job of the four. But then again, Alice didn't particularly fancy confronting Mark either, so all in all it wasn't too bad. "What about timing?"

"Charlie's class – the thirteen-two-and-under showjumping – is first," Mia said, studying the show programme. "My showing class follows that, and the Fratton Cup for Alice, Rosie and Mark is last. If he's intent on winning the Cup, he'll probably get to the show and start warming up just after my Ridden Show Pony class starts. He won't want to be hanging around for ages with a stolen pony, so I bet he'll leave it all to the last minute. So, we'll have to act after mine and Charlie's classes have finished and before the Cup starts."

Mia yawned as she finished speaking.

"That's settled, then," Charlie said, fighting back a yawn herself. "I doubt he'll get Moonlight out early – that way as few people as possible will spot him before he jumps. It won't give us much time to catch him."

"Let's just hope we have enough," Rosie said, opening her window wider and looking out into the still darkness to where the ponies were quietly dozing by the big tree. "It might be our only chance to reunite Poppy with her pony."

Rosie called Beanie, who scuttled up the stairs and snuffled around each of the girls' beds before settling down by Rosie's feet, with Pumpkin taking up position by her pillow. Charlie reached over to turn out the side light and the girls carried on talking for a while. Then Charlie and Alice whispered for a bit longer as Rosie, Mia and Beanie started to snore lightly. Gradually the room fell silent. The only sound inside Alice's head was her heart racing as she lay in the dark and started to panic in earnest about the Cup the next day.

Chapter Nine

THE cockerels woke Alice up after what felt like only five minutes of sleep. Once one started, a whole chorus followed, making further sleep impossible.

It was light and sunny outside, with the slight chill of early morning, when Alice rolled out of bed and walked over to the open window to see Scout in the paddock. Charlie was already up and dressed, jumping about excitedly. Mia sat up without a hair out of place, looking as perfect as she did when she'd got into bed. Rosie snorted and turned to face the wall, muttering something about Cups and refusals and just five more minutes.

Although Alice felt exhausted, she couldn't have gone back to sleep because her stomach had started churning. Once Rosie had finally been dragged out of bed, she and the others ate a full cooked breakfast served up by a sleepy Mrs Honeycott, but Alice only just managed to force down a glass of orange juice and half a slice of toast with home-made bramble jelly.

They dressed quickly in their old gear to get the ponies ready, and rushed out of the back door into the yard. They waved to Mr Honeycott and Will, who were already out in the fields looking at some of their free-range calves.

The sky was a perfect, cloudless blue – it was going to be a sweltering day. The ponies whickered noisily when the girls walked towards their paddock. Dancer was resting one front hoof on the bottom rung of the gate, excited about her breakfast.

As they slipped the ponies' headcollars on, Charlie suddenly cried out. Pirate had managed to rub his tail bandage off so that it was trailing round behind him, and the top of his tail hair was sticking out like a toilet brush. Alice was so nervous that she laughed far too loudly and earned herself a black look from Charlie.

Alice knew it was pretty hard to get a grey pony to shine like a chestnut or a bay, but Scout was ultra clean and his dapples stood out beautifully after she'd finished grooming him. Then she began to plait Scout's mane, and he dropped his head for her, shifting his weight and resting his off hind so that his hips were really angled. Alice wasn't very good at it and each plait got fatter and looser. It wasn't until right at the end that she remembered there was supposed to be an odd number of plaits up the neck, with one last one in the forelock making it even. Alice had ten by the time she reached Scout's ears, so she had to undo the last plait and hastily divide it into two weedy ones.

Once they were all finished grooming, they rushed back to the cottage to get changed into their show gear. Mia looked immaculate in her cream jods, her sparkling jodhpur boots, brown gloves and smart fitted black jacket. Her bright pink tie with silver spots was striking against her olive skin, her silky black hair tied back with a bright pink ribbon under her black velvet hat. She made the rest of them seem even shabbier than usual in their older, inexpensive jackets and slightly off-colour jods.

Back in the yard they fetched their tack, and Alice worried again about how slippery her polished saddle would be. Her fingers were shaking so much that she could hardly buckle the straps on the bridle or the girth. But finally, they were ready. When Mia pulled Wish out of the stable, the others gasped. The palomino mare, with her creamy mane and tail plaited, her dark eyes framed by her long fluttery eyelashes in her delicately curved dished head, looked even more incredible than usual. It would take a sensational pony to beat her into second place.

Charlie had battled heroically with Pirate's tail,

but it still looked like a curled-up hedgehog, and Dancer had even fatter plaits than Scout.

"Ready?" Mia asked as they all mounted. Rosie had an empty bucket and a bottle of Mia's pony shampoo ready for their plan proudly swinging over her arm.

Alice sat there for half a second before rapidly dismounting again. "Oooh, hang on a sec, I need the loo!"

As she dashed off, Rosie muttered. "Not again!"

Alice hurried back, trying to calm herself, but her legs had turned to jelly and she put the wrong foot into the stirrup before managing to get up, and they finally set off.

It only took fifteen minutes to hack along the lanes to the show, but if Alice thought the ride would calm her down she was wrong; her nerves were getting worse with every stride. They dismounted, loosened off their girths and headed straight for the secretary's tent to pick up their numbers as soon as they arrived.

"Mia, look," Rosie said as she found her name on the list and scanned down the rest. "Mark's name isn't on the list for the Fratton Cup!"

"Hmm, he must be planning to do a late entry," Mia mused, running her finger down the list to double-check. "That way he'll keep a low profile until the last second."

They didn't have much time to think about it though because it was nearly time for Charlie's class, the 13.2hh-and-under showjumping, and Charlie was one of the first to go. She rode over to the warm-up ring and started to walk, trot and canter an over-excited Pirate. He whizzed round the outside of the ring, terrorising any other pony that got too close, and flew over the practice jumps a few times before Charlie was called into the main ring for her round.

The others made their way to the edge of the rope marking off the ring. They watched as Pirate careered round, charging at each fence like a maniac. He even managed to take a stride out between the two fences in the double. Charlie sat quietly, anticipating Pirate's every stride, but the bay clonked the back pole and after that he knocked every fence, sending three more flying.

"Sixteen jumping faults for Charlie Hall riding her own Pirate," the judge announced over a crackly loudspeaker as Charlie rode out, smiling, to a smattering of claps.

"Not our lucky day." She shrugged, patting Pirate as she dismounted and gave him a handful of pony nuts from her pocket. She loosened her tie thankfully as the sun beat down, and Alice felt a twist in her stomach, wondering whether Charlie's bad start was going to set the tone for the rest of them. And for Poppy.

She didn't have long to wonder about fate, because as Charlie dismounted Mia said that it was time for her to start working in Wish for her showing class.

"Hang on a sec, is that who I think it is?" Charlie said, leaning over Pirate's saddle after loosening his girth, and squinting in the direction of the showground entrance. The others followed her gaze. Alice suddenly squeaked.

"It's Mark!" she said breathlessly, pointing to the far edge of the field. Mark's sleek, expensive horsebox was hard to miss, rolling in and bumping gently to a standstill among the other smaller, battered trailers.

"He's seriously early," Mia frowned, checking her watch. "The Fratton Cup doesn't start for at least an hour, and if Mark hasn't registered yet for the class he'll be one of the last to ride, after Alice."

Suddenly Mia wasn't sure what to do – she didn't want to miss her warm-up on Wish, but she couldn't miss seeing Mark bring Moonlight out of his horsebox either.

"I bet he keeps Moonlight in the box for ages, though," Rosie said. "I mean, he can't parade him round for too long before the class starts in case he gets recognised, even *with* a disguise. I reckon you'll have time to do your class first, Mia."

"I wouldn't be so sure," Charlie said suddenly. "Look, he's getting ready to open the ramp!"

"Quick!" Mia said urgently, feeling a rush of excitement and nerves over what they were about to do. "Time to get our plan under way. First things first – we need to find Poppy!"

The four of them looked round frantically, thrown by Mark's unexpectedly early appearance. For a moment Alice was convinced they'd never find Poppy in time and they'd miss their moment to reveal Moonlight. She had visions of Mark carrying the Cup away unchallenged. Then her legs wobbled at the thought of the Cup.

"There she is!" Charlie cried. She'd leaped back onto Pirate and was standing up in her stirrups, pointing over to the tea and lemonade tent.

"Right, Charlie, you take the ponies and I'll keep an eye on Mark. Rosie, fill your bucket and take up your position," Mia instructed. "Alice, you go and collect Poppy."

"Erm. Okay," Alice replied hesitantly.

"What now?" Mia asked testily.

"Um, can someone just keep an eye on Poppy for me for one sec?" Alice asked, dancing slightly on the spot.

"Where are you off to?" Mia hissed. "You can't disappear now!"

"Got to!" Alice replied, dashing towards the Portaloos for the fifth time.

When she got back Mia was gesturing at her wildly. Mark had lowered his ramp and was heading up it, disappearing inside the horsebox.

"Right, everyone – to your positions," Mia said, sounding very grand.

Alice scooted off towards Poppy, but when it came to approaching her, Alice suddenly realised that she hadn't even thought about what she was going to say. 'Hello Poppy, we've found Moonlight for you. Step this way'? Or how about, 'Poppy, Special Agent Alice Hathaway here. We've located your missing pony'? In the end she kept it simple.

"Poppy?" she said.

Poppy turned round. Her eyes looked haunted, and Alice could tell at once that losing Moonlight hadn't got any easier. Her face was pale and, although she smiled faintly, it was obviously difficult for her being surrounded by so many ponies when her own wasn't there. But not for long, Alice told herself.

"I, we, my friends and I, we think we may have something you might like to see."

Poppy looked puzzled but followed Alice back through the crowds. They stopped near Mark's horsebox. Only it was obvious at once that things weren't going according to plan, and Alice edged closer so that she could hear what they were saying. She had expected to walk over just in time to hear Mia declare her code word, see Rosie toss the water and Moonlight reappear right before Poppy's eyes.

Instead, Mia was looking cross and harassed while Mark was standing with one hand on his hip. In the other he was holding a lead rope, and at the end of that lead rope stood an exquisite pony. An exquisite *white* pony. Not only did this pony have one white back leg, it had three other white ones as well. Alice knew at once that no amount of soapy water could possibly transform this particular pony from white to white-with-lots-of-black-patches.

Mark's new pony was not Moonlight. Mark was not guilty as charged, and they'd nabbed the wrong culprit. But Mia seemed determined to ignore the glaringly obvious flaw in their case and desperately reeled off the clues from her notebook. When she had finished, Mark's lips curled into a nasty smile.

"So, you're the one who's been poking her nose into other people's business, are you? Harry told me and Dad all about you. Well, if you must know, this is the pony we've had our eye on; this is the proven winner Harry arranged for Dad to buy from a top showing contact of his at great cost, specially for this show." Mark turned and looked at his white pony smugly. "I wanted to keep Cloud Nine secret until today so that when I rode into that ring everyone would be totally wowed by him. I didn't want anyone to get wind of it beforehand, especially not the judge. This way we get maximum impact. I got fed up of losing in the jumping, and Ridden Show Pony seems like the easiest class in the world to win, so I reckon I've got this one stitched up. All I have to do is ride a few silly circles and the first prize will be mine. I'm not competing in the stupid Cup, so Poppy's not my rival this year; you are. Prepare to be beaten, Miss Busy Body."

Mia's mouth dropped open.

"But showing's not just about having the fanciest pony with the best conformation, you know," she pointed out furiously, feeling personally insulted by Mark's take on her and Wish's favourite class. "You need serious riding skills, too, to be able to school your pony to perfection. And you've got to be in harmony so that you can show off your pony's best bits, as well as looking totally, utterly smart, of course."

Mia shook her head. She was aware that other riders were starting to gather, pausing on their way past, listening in to their argument, but she didn't care. She narrowed her eyes. "We may not have got all our facts right, but there's one thing we were right about, and that's you, Mark. Whichever way you look at it, you're nothing but a cheat!"

At that moment, hearing the code word, Rosie charged round the corner of the box. She tripped on a clump of grass and, as she fell to the earth, flung the water bucket for all she was worth. Cloud Nine dodged to one side, and Mia ducked to the other. Taken by surprise, Mark didn't do either. He stayed exactly where he was. The water hit him full in the face, and he stood there, his smart showing jacket and jodhpurs drenched. Mark was speechless, spluttering in disbelief, as the watching group of riders gasped then started to giggle. Mia hadn't even meant to say the code word, but she'd blurted it out without thinking after hearing what he'd done. She held her hand to her mouth for a second before Rosie grabbed her, and they turned tail and ran, laughing like hyenas. At that moment Mark's dad walked around the horsebox, stopping in his tracks and looking furious that the pony he'd just bought at great expense to ensure victory was about to be ridden by a totally sodden rider.

"What happened here?" he asked, gobsmacked, as the little crowd dispersed.

"Isn't that obvious?!" Mark snapped, flinging the reins at his dad and stomping off towards the cab, dripping and squelching with every step.

Poppy turned to Alice. She'd been so transfixed by the unexpected turn of events that she'd almost forgotten Poppy was standing next to her.

"Is this what you wanted me to see? A water fight?" Poppy said. Alice opened her mouth to say something but she couldn't think what and closed it again. Poppy must have thought they were a bunch of halfwits.

But Poppy's pale face suddenly broke into a cheerful smile. "You've just made a very difficult day a teeny bit more cheerful," she beamed. "You know, last year Mark Tickle wouldn't even congratulate me on winning as we were lined up, he was so furious. I reckon he's got his just deserts for being so competitive! Thanks!"

With that, Poppy walked back to the tea tent to find her mum and wait for the Cup to start. As Alice joined the others, she was relieved that she hadn't told Poppy about them finding Moonlight. It would have been agonising for her to think he'd been found, only to have her hopes dashed the moment they'd been raised. After their burst of laughter, the others were now all looking as glum as Alice felt.

"Back to square one," Charlie said despondently.

"And not a single clue to help us," Mia said, studying her notebook.

"It's not as easy finding stolen ponies as we thought," Alice said, twiddling her pony tail absently. "I haven't the foggiest where we go from here – has anyone else?"

Mia sighed. "I'm not sure there is anywhere to go from here."

"Good shot of mine with the water, though," Rosie said proudly.

"Anyway, you better get warmed up," Charlie suddenly said, handing Mia Wish's reins. "You're running late – you'll be called into the ring soon."

Mia flipped shut her notebook and handed it to Charlie with a sigh before tightening Wish's girth and jumping into the saddle. The girls wished her luck as she trotted her pony over to the warm-up area. They knew Mia had left herself short of time to prepare, something she'd never done before, but for once winning was not Mia's top priority.

The other three headed over to a large ring near the far side of the field. There was a huge horse chestnut tree just beside it, and they gratefully slumped down in the shade waiting for Mia and her fellow competitors to be called in together. Their ponies grazed contentedly, raising their heads every once in a while to look out over the showground.

They didn't have to wait long before Mia rode into the ring with another nine ponies following her. They started off by walking, trotting and cantering in a group, then all lined up in the centre of the ring. The judge walked up to each of them in turn and inspected them, then sent them out for their individual shows. The girls watched silently as Wish moved effortlessly and gracefully around the ring, her neck rounded and her toes flicking out with each step. She captivated the scattered crowd in her electric pink velvet browband, which matched Mia's tie. It didn't matter that Mia had been a bit rushed in her preparation – she still looked perfect and rode supremely, with Wish looking as stunning as ever.

They held their breath as Mark began his individual show on his newly purchased, top-level show pony, Cloud Nine. As the pony moved, it was as if his hooves floated above the ground. But Mark had a face like thunder. He sullenly kicked and pulled Cloud Nine about during his individual show and the pony, used to more delicate handling, showed his resentment with a few well-timed bucks and shakes of his head. Not only that, but Mark was still drying out from the soaking Rosie had given him earlier; his leather boots looked dull and unpolished and his red tie had drooped. He was not amused. Nor was the judge as she got the ponies lined back up again.

She stopped in front of Mia and had a few words. Then the judge moved on and halted in front of Mark. Even from where the girls were standing they could hear the judge's high-pitched voice floating across on the warm air.

"Absolute disgrace. What have you been doing? Apple bobbing? This is supposed to be a serious show, you know. You've let this wonderful pony, which looks awfully familiar to me, down thoroughly, and for absolutely no reason that I can fathom."

The judge walked to the next pony, a pretty bright bay, and spent some time praising pony and rider highly. Then the judge called Mia out first ahead of the pretty bay, with a furious Mark unplaced.

As Mia received her red rosette, Mark stomped out and the girls jumped up, cheering loudly. They rushed forward to congratulate Mia, who leaned down to hug Wish warmly.

"At least one thing's gone according to plan today," Charlie said as the tannoy crackled into life.

"Can all the riders for our final class of the day, the Fratton Cup, please make their way to the main ring to walk the course."

Alice remembered the Cup again with a jolt, and went from being filled with happiness for

Mia to being filled with a gazillion butterflies. Her stomach flipped as she and Rosie handed their reins to Charlie and Mia. With knocking knees, she made her way to the ring on foot.

Rosie kept looking out for plants by the fences that Dancer might take a fancy to, distracting Alice so much that she forgot whether it was a right or a left turn after the planks and whether the triple bar followed the double or the oxer, making her more nervous than ever. As other riders walked purposefully past her – including Tallulah Starr, loudly counting out her strides – Alice panicked, thinking she'd never remember the course.

She strode out the distances between fences, imagining Scout's canter stride in her mind. As she walked the path she'd soon be riding, her heart raced faster and faster. Up close, the fences looked solid, tall and wide. Most of them were three feet high, and the triple bar, the last fence, was over three feet wide. She felt as if she must be turning green as they headed back out to the others, and was sure she'd forget which course to take and let Scout down.

Rosie was the first to go. Charlie gave her a leg-up into the saddle and Dancer's ears flopped out sideways, her eyes goggling.

"Good luck!" Charlie called out as Rosie flapped around, trying to get Dancer towards the warm-up ring. "See you when you get back."

"I doubt I'll be gone long," Rosie reasoned. "Dancer doesn't feel in a going mood today, so I don't think we'll get far round the course."

Alice was one of the last in, and much as she wanted to put off the moment as long as possible, she secretly envied the fact that Rosie would soon have her round over and done with.

The others gave the ponies a drink of water each from Rosie's bucket, which had been thoroughly rinsed out, then went over to the ring to watch Rosie jump.

"Rosie Honeycott, riding Dancer," the judge announced as Rosie entered.

Dancer's plaits had started to come undone, and the strawberry roan mare cantered towards the first fence, a brush, very suspiciously, and ground to a halt in front of it. The others all groaned. Rosie turned Dancer, shook her up and, shouting encouragement, trotted back to the fence, and this time the mare heaved herself over. After that, Dancer seemed to take heart and jumped the next three fences almost on the move, but she ground to a halt at the gate before cat-leaping over and refusing to have anything to do with the double that followed. The claxon sounded.

"Rosie Honeycott and Dancer are eliminated," the judge announced.

Rosie rode out beaming.

"What are you looking so happy for? You only made it to fence six!" Mia pointed out, wondering how anyone could be so delighted with such a performance.

"But that's five more than last year! At this rate

we might have a hope of reaching the last fence next time! That's serious progression!" Rosie exclaimed, showering Dancer with pats and kisses as Tallulah Starr cantered past into the ring on one of her many grey ponies, Diamond Starr. As Rosie slid out of the saddle, the puffing mare gobbled up the mints Rosie had brought with her.

Rosie, Charlie and Mia looked towards Alice.

"You better start getting ready," Mia said. "It'll be your turn soon."

Alice gulped, loudly.

Chapter Ten

ALICE felt herself go pale and weak as she mounted. She patted Scout and rode off by herself. Quietly, she warmed Scout up in trot and canter. His ears kept flickering back, as if he could tell that she was nervous and wanted to check she was okay. When they were both ready to go over a practice fence, Alice heard a loud voice barking orders.

She looked up after checking her girth and saw Daisy ride past, closely followed by a glowering Major Thurlow. Alice frowned. Daisy was the last to go in the class, but she'd left herself hardly any time to warm Shadow up. Alice was about to call out hello when the Major glared at her.

"No distractions today, young lady. I don't want my daughter falling off because of you again," he growled, before turning his attention back to Daisy. "Now, don't fuss that pony about, bring him over a fence, let him know you mean business!"

Daisy looked thoroughly miserable, cantering away lopsidedly around the practice ring. She turned Shadow towards the warm-up fence, but her reins were so baggy that the pony ran past the poles without even attempting to jump. Daisy just about managed to cling on, but the Major roared at her to try again.

Turning her concentration back to Scout, Alice trotted over the cross pole a couple of times. She completely failed to see a stride first time but Scout popped over, waiting for her to catch up with him. After the fence had been put up to a decent upright, Alice rode over a couple more times. With her hands still shaking and her legs as useless as jelly, she rode towards the exit of the warm-up area. Daisy looked over as Alice headed out.

"Good luck!" Alice called, giving her an encouraging smile. Daisy looked as if she was about to say something, but the Major was by her side in a shot and she looked away again.

As Alice, her teeth chattering, waited just outside the ring to be called, Rosie announced that there had been no clear rounds so far, not even by Tallulah Starr. "That means if you can go clear, Alice, you'll win. You've only got Daisy behind you, and there's no way she'll leave everything up. She probably won't even remember the course. You can do it!"

"Break a leg!" Mia said.

Alice groaned.

"I can't do it," she whispered faintly. "I can't go in! If there are no clears yet the course must be awful!"

Charlie stepped up, her face stern as she pushed her hat back on her head to look at Alice properly.

"Alice, you have faced the wrath of Harry Franklin, you went back to his yard, alone and unaided. If you can do that, if you can hide in the back of a stable in the line of duty, not knowing whether you're going to escape with your life, you can jump a course of piddly show jumps."

"Quick, the judge has called your name three times!" Rosie cried. "You better get going if you're still going to jump!"

As the judge called out their names a final time, and with Charlie's rallying cry rattling in her ears, Alice pressed Scout forward into canter and they entered the ring. Alice saw Poppy look up at her and smile as she rode past. It hit Alice then that at least she had a pony to jump. She had to do this, for Poppy, for Moonlight and for Scout.

Alice took a huge, deep breath and waited for the bell to ring. As soon as it sounded, Alice cantered an arc and headed towards the brush fence. Charlie was right, Alice thought, facing Harry *was* more frightening than this.

She pushed on strongly, suddenly filled with an extraordinary zest and as a result over-jumped the brush fence and nearly shot straight past the second, the gate. But Scout saw it just in time and twisted over it, tucking his hooves up, desperate not to touch it.

With her newfound confidence they were gaining speed with every stride, and they jumped over the first part of the double too big, landing close to the second part, but Scout was clever and took a half stride before flying out over the parallel.

After that Alice started to calm down. Scout's ears were pricked, looking for each new fence but flickering back as she asked him to turn left and right through the twisty course. He soared over each fence, bunching up and popping over the tricky planks and stretching his neck low over the wider spreads. As they flew over the wall only the huge, wide triple bar stood between them and a clear round, between Alice and the Fratton Cup.

Scout thundered up to it. Everything in the ring fell silent except the beat of his hooves on the dry grass. Alice kept her legs on her pony's sides and her hands soft; Scout met it perfectly and launched into the air. He snapped his hooves up and dropped his neck, arcing beautifully. Alice crouched low over Scout, just out of the saddle, and it felt as if they were suspended in the air for hours, reaching for the distant back pole that seemed impossibly far away.

Alice heard a clout and the crowd gasped. Then they were plunging down to earth again. Scout pitched slightly on landing and Alice shot up his neck, seeing the grass coming up towards her for a moment before getting her balance and sitting back in the saddle as the crowd burst into wild cheers and applause. Alice twisted round – the back pole was rocking slightly, but it stayed up! They'd gone clear!

Alice patted Scout wildly, praising him aloud as they shot out of the ring at a rapid trot. She felt herself going bright pink as the relief hit her, along with Charlie and Rosie as they congratulated her heartily. Mia's face broke into a broad smile.

Suddenly Alice felt that she had conquered the world, and it was the best feeling she'd ever had.

As Daisy waited alongside them to ride into the ring, looking pale green with worried eyes, Charlie said, "Of course, what I said before you went in about you being a hero and all that, well it was only partly true. I mean, you may have performed heroics while trying to locate a stolen pony, but you still failed. Like the rest of us. But if it helped get you round…"

Alice threw her stick at Charlie. She was only joking, but Alice looked across and saw Poppy watching Scout and felt the failure of the case even more, despite the elation that was flooding through her. Suddenly it felt like the lead weight was sitting in her stomach again. Imagine losing Scout after he put in that round, after winning a class like the Fratton Cup.

Alice racked her brains as she jumped down and loosened Scout's girth, pulling off her black jacket and tie while Mia fed Scout almost a whole packet of mints. There *must* be something more that they could do, something that they had overlooked in their evidence! Alice went over it in her head one more time, but her mind drew a blank. Rosie offered Scout some water from her replenished bucket, which he sloshed around before drinking deeply, slurping and dripping it all over Alice's white shirt, not that she cared.

"That cup's as good as yours," Charlie said as the bell rang for Daisy's round.

They watched as Shadow cantered towards the first fence and jumped it so big that Daisy landed up his neck. She managed to cling on, pulled the reins and aimed him at the gate. Again, Shadow over-jumped, alive now that he was in the ring. This time Daisy got left behind, almost being bumped out of the saddle onto the pony's black rump.

But it was at the third fence that the drama really began. Daisy leaned to the left to help turn the charging Shadow. As she did so, her whole body began to lean and it became obvious that her saddle was slipping. Typical! She hadn't remembered to tighten her girth, even for the Fratton Cup! The crowd let out loud oohs and ahhs as Daisy miraculously stayed on for another three fences until, as she approached the double, she turned Shadow and gravity took over. She slipped further and further as Shadow cantered eagerly around the edge of the ring, unchecked, before he finally deposited Daisy on the grass with a heavy thud. Daisy let out an audible sigh, then lay there watching the sky, leaving Shadow to thunder out of the ring, scattering the crowd in his path.

Alice couldn't help noticing as Shadow shot past, stirrups flying, that there was something unusual in the way that Daisy had parted company with her pony. Normally Shadow was crafty, and he bucked, dropped a shoulder or ducked out of a fence in a deliberate attempt to dislodge his rider. The loose girth merely added to Daisy's problems. But today Daisy had *only* fallen because the saddle had slipped. Shadow was still going straight as a die and had almost looked surprised when he saw Daisy disappear beneath him.

While Alice tried to work out why that bothered her, there was still the matter of Shadow running riot around the showground. A crowd had gathered around Daisy, thinking she might have drawn her last breath. But Alice had seen her fall like that a hundred times and knew that she'd be fine. She'd be lying there contemplating the cloud formation before getting up with a sigh and carrying on as if nothing had happened, so Alice decided to go and catch Shadow.

She threw Scout's reins to Rosie and sprinted off in pursuit of the black pony. Alice wasn't quite sure why she was so determined to be the one to catch him, but she was determined nonetheless. And she wasn't the only one. Alice looked to her left and noticed the Major, red-faced and puffing, racing her. Alice accelerated and noticed the

Major try to do the same. She frowned and sprinted ahead. She was sure the Major would be less than happy with Shadow when he caught up with the black pony, and she wanted to make sure she got there first. She glanced over her shoulder and saw the Major come to a puffing halt, bending double with his hands on his knees as he tried to catch his breath.

Alice raced over to the far corner of the field where Shadow had pulled himself up. She prepared herself for the pony being a weasel, remembering him crunching her finger between his lightning-quick teeth last time she'd tried to grab him. But instead he let her catch up his reins without even attempting the smallest of nips or flattening of ears. In fact, he nuzzled her. Maybe it was the heat, but this pony wasn't acting like Shadow at all, Alice thought as she started to lead him back to the others. His first few steps were reluctant, and then she remembered the saddle hanging under his belly. Alice undid the girth and caught it before it fell to the ground.

She wiped her hand across her face, boiling hot after running in the heat, then put the saddle back on. She took the reins again and jogged Shadow over to Charlie, Rosie and Mia, who had run to meet her halfway across the showground.

Alice was about to tell them about Shadow's transformed nature when she noticed Mia looking disgusted.

"What on earth have you been doing?" Mia asked. "What's all that black gunk smeared over your face, and your shirt come to that?!"

"What gunk? What are you going on about?! All I've done is get Shadow!" Alice retorted, wiping her face and inspecting a darkly smudged hand.

It suddenly dawned on her. Alice turned slowly to the pony she was still holding and gave him another pat. Alice looked at her hand. It was as black as her boots, and her heart started to race.

"Yuk!" Rosie squealed. "What is it?"

"I don't believe it!" Mia added, taking off her

brown gloves and sliding a finger down the pony's neck before inspecting it. "It's *dye*!"

"What, you mean…?" Rosie stuttered.

Alice and Mia nodded wildly, as Charlie whooped. But after their last mistake, they had to be truly sure that it was dye and not some mad mix-up with shampoo and boot polish that Daisy had made while grooming. Mia flipped open her notebook with shaking fingers and studied the photo from the missing ad.

"Right. We know that Shadow's all black, he hasn't got a hair of white anywhere on him. Moonlight, on the other hand, has a black head but there's a white star on his forehead."

With that Mia stepped forward and amazed the other three when she pulled out the end of her precious pink tie and began to wipe between the pony's eyes. The pony dropped his head and blinked softly, leaning into her and enjoying the fuss as the other three danced on the spot impatiently.

After a few minutes, Mia stopped rubbing and held the pony's forelock out of the way. They all gasped. There, in the middle of his forehead – it was unmistakable! It might have been murky, but it was *definitely* a white star.

"Moonlight!" Rosie gasped.

"We've found him!" Charlie laughed, hugging Alice.

"They must have been seriously desperate to win," Alice said, laughing in disbelief.

"I *thought* Shadow's coat looked patchy when we bumped into Daisy on that ride the other day," Mia said. "It wasn't because her grooming skills were shoddy after all – she must have been riding Moonlight, with this gunky dye over all his white bits!"

"And Daisy's house is close enough to Hawthorn Farm, Moonlight's yard, for her and the Major to walk him back there in the middle of the night," Charlie added.

They heard a cough and turned to see the

Major, puce and still out of breath, stalking towards them.

"Ah, now, I'll take Shadow from you if you don't mind," he said, trying to sound friendly.

He made a lunge for the reins. Alice moved them quickly out of his reach. The Major forced a smile.

"Come on now, hand him over, be a sport, he *is* my daughter's pony, after all," the Major said through gritted teeth.

"Dad, forget it, they've worked it out."

The Major whipped round to see Daisy standing behind him, looking at the ground, her black jacket dusty but otherwise apparently none the worse for her fall.

"Stop talking nonsense, Daisy," the Major bluffed, edging towards Moonlight. "You must have had a knock to the head! We'd better take the pony and get you home *quickly* so you can have a lie down."

"I spend most of my life lying down after

falling off Shadow, in case you hadn't noticed," Daisy pointed out crossly, finally squaring her shoulders and standing up to him. "I don't need to lie down again now! And I won't go along with your plan any more. Do you realise what you've done? You wanted me to win so badly, just so I could be more like you, that you stole – yes *stole* – the one pony you thought would guarantee me victory around the Cup course. I couldn't believe it when I discovered Moonlight hidden in one of our stables. But it wouldn't have mattered which pony you'd put me on. I still wouldn't give a stuff about competing or winning."

The Major tried to speak but Daisy silenced him. Mia nodded her approval.

"Face it, Dad, I'm just not like you," Daisy said, jutting out her chin defiantly. "I'm me."

The Major glanced uneasily at the girls, then turned to Daisy. "Really? You're *sure* you don't like competing," he said urgently, in a hushed voice. "Not just a little bit? Because I'm convinced that with more drilling over fences you'll turn into a fine show jumper yet!"

"Dad!" Daisy exclaimed, going slightly pink. "I never want to jump another fence again! Ever!"

The Major looked seriously disgruntled and his moustache twitched irritably. He hummed and hawed awkwardly for a few seconds, then puffed out his cheeks and thwacked his shiny boots with his stick.

"I see," he finally tutted, clearing his throat and adjusting his tie. "In that case, I suppose I have some apologising to do."

At that moment one of the judges bustled over to them, looking slightly cross.

"Come on, dear," she said to Alice, pulling her arm. "It's very good of you to go gallivanting off after the loose pony, but we have to make the presentation for the Cup. We've been calling your for ages. Chop chop."

Alice hurried along behind her, leading Moonlight. The others followed, trotting their ponies in hand. Daisy was behind them, smiling triumphantly as she walked alongside the red-faced, grumbling Major. As they reached the main ring, Alice looked over and could see the Fratton Cup set out on a trestle table nearby. It was so nearly hers. She caught the others all looking at her, wondering what she would do. But Alice knew there was only one thing she could do. She quickly dodged to the judges' cabin, the others following. She held on to the end of Moonlight's reins as she ducked inside. After she'd had a quick word with the judge, the tannoy crackled into action. Alice cleared her throat and the sound system whined.

"The class isn't finished yet," she announced, desperately searching for Poppy in the sea of people as she spoke. A murmur rippled through the spectators, sending a buzz through the crowd as they wondered what the hold-up was. "There's still one more rider to jump in the first round!"

Alice whispered something to the judge,

whose eyebrows shot up in surprise. As Alice ducked back out to join the others standing by the cabin, the judge leaned forward towards the microphone.

"And that rider is..." the judge hesitated for a moment, then took a deep breath and continued. "That rider is Poppy Brookes."

Poppy started as her name echoed round the ring. She stared at the girls, who were waving wildly at her to come down, then pointing towards the black pony. She shaded her eyes from the late afternoon sun, leaning forward to get a better look. Suddenly her face lit up and she gasped, her hand coming up to her mouth. Quick as a flash, she dodged her way through the excited, confused crowd then raced as fast as she could, skidding to a breathless stop in front of the black pony. Alice held the reins out to her. Poppy started to laugh, but it turned into a cry as she stepped forward, hardly daring to believe what was happening.

"You've still got to jump your pony," Alice said, trying to keep her voice steady. "You've still got to jump Moonlight."

Chapter Eleven

POPPY saw the black dye on Mia's tie and Alice's face. Moonlight nickered excitedly, his nostrils fluttering as he stepped forwards and rubbed his head against her. She threw her arms around his neck, burying her head in his mane. The crowd stood in stunned silence as they watched the pony turn his head and encircle Poppy, as if he were hugging her back, then a collective 'ahh' rang out through the stands.

With a sniff, Poppy took a step back, shaking her head and laughing as if she still couldn't believe it. She was covered now with the black sticky dye, but she didn't care. She set the saddle straight, tightened the girths and jumped up. She was wearing jodhpurs already, and Mia quickly took off her riding hat and passed it to her. Reunited, Moonlight and Poppy cantered into the ring as if in a dream.

"Well, it's a bit unconventional, I must say!" the judge announced over the blaring tannoy. "But we now have the last competitor in the ring for the Fratton Cup. Please give a very big hand for Poppy Brookes, riding her *very own* Moonlight."

The crowd gave the pair a roar of approval. Poppy and Moonlight, both looking as excited as each other, flew over each fence, one by one, until they'd cleared the last with inches to spare.

Alice was clapping wildly until Charlie looked at her ruefully and shouted over the din, "You know what that means, don't you?"

"Jump off!" the judge declared over the crackling loud speaker. "Alice Hathaway and Scout to jump first."

In all the excitement, Alice had forgotten about the fact that there was still a competition going on. Despite all Charlie's motivating advice,

Alice was all over the place as she tried to memorise the new, shortened course, which was going to be against the clock. Once the fences were rearranged and she'd warmed up Scout again, they rode back into the ring.

But as the bell rang, her mind went blank and Alice cantered a whole lap of the ring before she heard Charlie shouting out "Gate!" and the course flooded back. Alice turned Scout on a sixpence and he obligingly took off neatly, then raced on to the double, clearing it easily before turning back to the parallel and twisting to the wall, then charging on to the triple bar. Scout flew it, and this time Alice managed a more dignified landing.

She rode out to loud cheers, patting Scout over and over, pulling his ears gently. He bounced underneath the saddle, his ears pricked, full of beans and pleased with himself.

Alice knew but didn't really care that she'd dithered about at the start while the stopwatch was ticking. When Poppy came in and whizzed round in half the time, she received a burst of foot-stomping applause from everyone, none more so than the four girls standing by the entrance. As she lined up afterwards in the centre of the ring to collect her rosette, Alice turned and beamed at Poppy, who walked Moonlight over to her, leaned over and gave her a tight hug. Even though Alice had dreamed of winning the Fratton Cup, she couldn't have wished for anything more special at that moment than coming second.

"Congratulations!" Alice shouted above the standing ovation as Poppy was presented with the big silver cup. She wasn't sure whether she meant it for Moonlight or for winning the Cup, but she meant it nonetheless.

They set off at a fast canter around the ring, with Scout's blue second-placed rosette streaming from his bridle. Normally the winner leads the victory parade, but Poppy dropped back so that Moonlight and Scout were racing stride for stride alongside each other, the two girls laughing as the ponies galloped with their ears pricked, clearly enjoying themselves.

After two circuits of the ring they both charged out, and Alice finally managed to pull Scout up by Charlie, Rosie and Mia. Alice quickly jumped down from the saddle and loosened Scout's girth. As Rosie held out a bucket of water for Scout, the other two patted Alice on the back. After Scout had made them all squeal by dribbling over everyone, they heard hoof beats and looked up.

Poppy was leading Moonlight over, holding the cup. She lifted it towards them.

"I want you to have it," she said, looking from Alice to the others. "I couldn't have won it without all of you. It belongs to you. I can't begin to put into words how I feel about having Moonlight back here safe again when I thought I'd lost him for ever. I just can't thank you enough for finding him."

Alice looked at the cup. It was her biggest

ambition to win it, but she wanted to do it properly. Besides, she was over the moon with her second place – her jumping round had gone better than she could ever have dared to dream of when she'd woken up that morning. And seeing Poppy standing there beaming, she knew that restoring Moonlight to her was more important than any cup ever could be. Even the Fratton Cup.

"No, it's okay. It's yours, you keep it. Moonlight was the star of the show. You both won it fair and square," Alice said.

Poppy beamed.

"Okay, but on one condition," she replied. "You tell me all about how you found Moonlight and how he got into *this* sticky mess!"

The girls hastily filled Poppy in. Just as they finished, they heard someone clearing his throat behind them. They turned to see Daisy standing next to the Major, who was looking rather red and awkward. He blustered for a second, suitably shamefaced, before Daisy elbowed him.

"Poppy," she said determinedly, "Dad has got something to say to you, and your parents."

"We'll leave you to it," Mia said, smiling at Daisy just as Poppy's parents walked over to join Poppy, Daisy and the Major.

As they walked away, Alice glanced over her shoulder and saw Poppy standing with her arm over Moonlight's neck, her pony relaxed and contentedly cropping some grass. Her blue, second-placed rosette ribbons fluttered in her face. She wanted this day, this show, to last for ever, but it was time to get the ponies back. The girls tightened their ponies' girths, mounted and headed for the show exit. They rode back to Blackberry Farm feeling exhausted but happy.

"How amazing was that? We well and truly solved that mystery!" Alice said, feeling quite professional and important as they turned off the lane into the woods. "We were like proper detectives!"

"Pony detectives, more like," Rosie replied.

"*That's* what we should call ourselves!" Charlie exclaimed. "The Pony Detectives!"

The four girls looked round at each other, suddenly excited.

"It's perfect!" Mia said. She couldn't help smiling, even though she wished she'd been the one to have come up with the name.

"I wonder what our next case will involve?" Alice sighed happily as they walked their ponies through the wooded path on long reins, their feet dangling out of the stirrups.

"Kidnapping and ransom notes?" Charlie said hopefully, leaning down to give Pirate a hug.

"Or a world-famous dressage horse who's vanished without a trace?" Mia added, closing her eyes as they wandered along.

"Oh, hang on! We forgot something!" Rosie suddenly exclaimed.

"What?" Alice asked lazily, feeling the warmth of the sun coming through the trees.

"We forgot to ask Poppy about a reward!"

"Rosie!" they all groaned.

At that exact same moment Dancer caught sight of a tempting leafy bush at the side of the path. She lunged, pulling Rosie so far out of the saddle that she slid head first down Dancer's neck, over her ears, and landed with a thud, startling the other ponies. They dived in different directions, and before they knew what had happened the girls were all sitting in a messy heap on the mossy earth.

The ponies stopped a couple of strides away and stood looking down at them quizzically. Pirate stomped his hoof.

"I was only saying!" Rosie explained as she stood up and pulled Dancer out of the offending shrub, trailing great long leaves.

As Rosie turned round she was grinning from ear to ear, just like the rest of her friends.

The Pony Detectives had a feeling that this summer holiday was going to be the best one ever. And it had only just begun.

Mia's Top Grooming Tips

Rosie wonders why I'm so fussy about grooming, but, as I keep telling her, it:

- helps get rid of loose hair and dirt
- is a chance to check for any lumps or bumps
- helps your pony's circulation.

So, put on your pony's headcollar and tie him up with a quick-release knot, then you're ready to begin!

Hoof pick
Use a pick to scrape out stones or muck from your pony's hooves. Start at the heel and move round to the toe.

Mane comb
Comb your pony's mane and forelock nice and flat. (Impossible for Pirate!) A soft body brush is great for this too.

Rubber curry comb
Start grooming at the top of your pony's neck and work back to his tail on both sides. A rubber curry comb helps to lift loose hair.

Dandy brush

A dandy brush is for getting rid of dried mud. It's quite a stiff brush, so don't use it on your pony's bony or tickly bits.

Body brush

Gently brush your pony's face, then his body. This brush removes grease, so don't use it if your pony lives in the field all the time – he'll need that grease to waterproof his coat.

Cloth stable rubber

Wipe a stable rubber over your pony's coat to get rid of any surface dust. It'll give him that extra sparkle!

Hoof oil

For special occasions, brush on some hoof oil to make your pony's hooves shine.

MIA'S STAR TIP
Give your pony lots of hugs while you groom and tell him how lovely he is. It's great bonding time!

The Pony Detectives' Guide to Tacking Up!

Before you begin, tie up your pony with a quick-release knot.

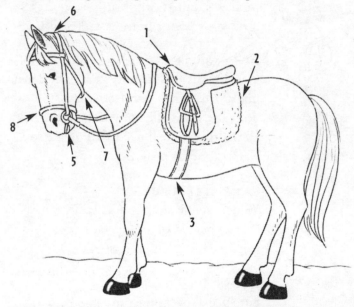

1 Put his saddle on (gently, so it doesn't flump down and startle him) then slide it back until it's in the right spot.

2 Check that the numnah, which sits under the saddle, isn't wrinkled – it's not very comfy for your pony.

3 Fasten the girth. Check it's nice and tight before and after you mount, or you might end up on the floor like Daisy!

4 Grab your bridle and stand next to your pony's head, facing forwards. Hold the bridle about halfway down in your right hand and rest that same hand on your pony's nose.

5 Use your left hand to guide the bit into your pony's mouth. Be careful not to clonk the metal bit on his teeth!

6 Slip the headpiece over your pony's ears. (You might have to stand on tiptoe!)

7 Do up the throat lash and then the noseband **(8)**.

MIA'S STAR TIP

Put your thumb into the side of your pony's mouth to encourage him to open up – he hasn't got teeth there, so it won't hurt!

Then, when you're all tacked up, give your pony plenty of praise!

Alice's Guide to Jumps and Fences

Brush

A brush fence is made of rustic poles with upright twiggy bits.

Cross pole

The best fence to warm up over! Its higher sides encourage ponies to jump at the centre.

Upright

The upright has poles or planks positioned one above the other.

Wall

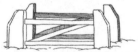

Gate

The wall and the gate are upright fences that don't use poles.

Parallel oxer

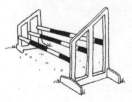

This is a spread fence, made up of two uprights of the same height placed close together.

Ascending oxer

The back upright on an ascending oxer is higher than the one at the front.

Triple bar

Scout's favourite! The poles in this spread fence get higher from the front to the back. Ponies can really stretch out over these.

The Fratton Cup Course

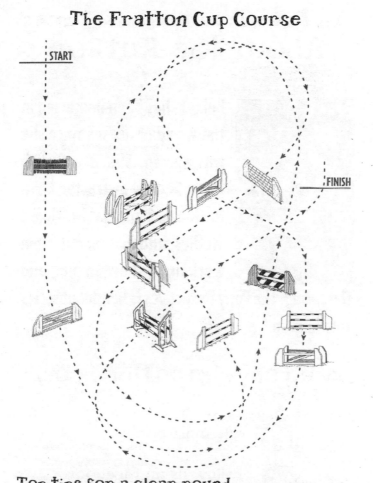

Top tips for a clear round

- Walk the course so you know which way to ride.
- Warm up your pony, but don't over-jump him!
- Once you're in the ring, wait for the bell before you start.
- As you're jumping one fence, look out for the next.
- Heap praise on your pony as you ride through the finish!

About the Author

Belinda has been immersed in the world of horses since she was eleven. She is a British Horse Society Instructor, has a National Diploma in Horse Studies and has spent time working in showjumping and flat racing. The Pony Detectives is her debut series for children.

www.pony-detectives.co.uk

 @templarbooks

 Follow us on Facebook:
facebook.com/templarfiction

templar publishing
www.templarco.co.uk